Catharsis

By Matthew O'Neil

HYPATIA PRESS

Published by Hypatia Press in the United States in 2020

ISBN: 978-1-83919-329-3

Cover design by Claire Wood

www.hypatiapress.org

For Katie

1

"Fuck off, you cunt!"

The scream echoed off the house across the street.

"I'm out for a week and you turn into the town bicycle? What have I—"

"How dare you!" a woman's voice hollered back. "I did no such thi—"

"No such thing?" A dish shattered. "Explain the hang up phone calls! Explain the slow driving cars past our house…"

"You paranoid loser!"

Jude stood outside his house, backpack slung over his shoulders. There was a heavy feeling in his chest and a lump in his throat. His hands were clutching the straps of his bag with white knuckles. His toes twiddled in his shoes; they looked like engines turning, but the emergency brake was on. Learning to pop the knuckles of his toes helped to distract him, process thoughts, and stay focused in class.

None of it helped when Jude got home. He could still hear his parents yelling.

"This loser pays the fucking mortgage so you can prance around the house in your lingerie to entice—"

"Once, I did that! And it was while I was waiting for you, asshole!"

"Don't blame me! You barely touch me as it is, but you're on display for all…"

"Get over yourself, Jacob!"

Another crash.

Jude shuffled one foot forward, only to draw it back. Rapid clicking, like toy gunfire, started getting louder. Turning to see two students from the middle school riding toward him on their bikes, his heart raced.

Please don't hear this. Please don't stop, Jude thought.

Bringing his attention back down toward his feet, he forced them to move. A jack hammer slammed against his sternum as sweat started to drip down his back. Making it to the base of the concrete steps, one foot up, the clicks just behind him, another crash stabbed through the placid air. Then squealing brakes. Tears that Jude had been successful in holding back, almost every time he came home to catastrophes like this, gushed down his cheeks.

"What the fuck is going on there?" one of the boys asked, his voice quivering.

"Scarowsky house," the other said, as though reciting a dirge. "Happens a lot."

Jude's body flooded with cold shakes. His muscles ached with tension. A fire lit in his calves, and he hopped up the steps two at a time. Swinging open the door, Jude dropped his bag, hearing light ethereal notes and scrapings as the bag slammed on the floor. Cracks and scrapes sounded off as he bounded for the stairs up to his room. He knew all too well, after one bad entrance, that taking his shoes off at the door wasn't the best idea. Even if his parents weren't in the middle of a fight upon his arrival, they might have both taken off to go to their respective lawyer's, or mother's, house to vent. These messes were usually cleaned up after they both had a few bottles of wine in them. Jude twisted and dropped, sitting at the top of the stairs, frantically tugging at the heels of his shoes.

"All you fucking care about is sex!" Jude heard his mother scream.

"It's not about sex!" his dad snarled. "It's about you having sex with every guy but the one you promised yourself to!"

"It's the last thing on my mind!"

"After getting it from every other guy in town, I can see why!"

"Get the fuck out of my house!"

"Your house? YOUR house?"

Jude's shoes rocketed off his feet, thumping down the steps in clumsy gymnastics moves. He launched himself up and bolted into his room. Slamming the door behind him, he took the hook on the door frame and slid it into the metal hoop on the edge of the door. His face, hot and damp with a mixture of tears and sweat, contorted into aguish.

The couple kept fighting, but the words were muffled. It was a rare day for them. Usually the fights ended after one broken thing, be it a mirror, window, or dish. All the stops were pulled. Jude's father had gotten home before him, meaning he left work early to confront his mother.

In a small town, your business becomes everyone else's. But if the wrong person saw it, your business—no matter how innocent—could be made into tabloid news. Jude's father couldn't seem to tell the difference.

Jude's breath was rapid, feeling like an elephant was sitting on his chest. His heart rate felt more like a vibration in the more intense moments. Each muscle, every fiber, felt so tense and tough that a slight poke might cause his skin to snap off like a bursting balloon. Jude felt the spraying of his innards all over the wall might produce the most cathartic consequence for these anxious times.

The thoughts though.

It's never going to end.

You're not worthy.

Only someone as weak as you would feel like this.

What's the point?

If it's not them, they'll turn the anger on you!

Just give up.

Jude jumped up from the floor and slammed the power switch on his Super Nintendo. With a loud snap, the company logo appeared on the screen, accompanied by the familiar toy chime. And when the Super

Mario World theme started beeping through the small TV on his desk, the anxiety started to melt. It was like taking the first taste of a summer ice cream cone, or stepping inside during the frigid winters with the fireplace burning. It meant comfort. It meant familiarity. It meant an escape from the world.

Coated with a light, slick greasiness from hours of gameplay, Jude's hands found their familiar placement around the controller, and his sobs had subsided into light, intermittent gasps. This was where he found his happiness. An escape from the war zone beneath him. Selecting one of the files that had not been played, it was days like these that he needed a longer commitment to his games. He needed to start with easier, familiar territory that he knew he could beat. With formulaic challenges, and with the easy settings of earlier stages, these levels felt to Jude the way he was sure a few glasses of wine felt to his father. Certainly, challenges lay ahead. What better way to prepare for them than to turn to what was familiar and comforting? Those quick accomplishments elevated his mood and made him feel capable. It was a distraction, and perhaps one that would later lead to disappointment or a melt down upon facing a challenge that was more difficult. It was more important to get the win in earlier to stop the stabbing in his chest and head... Especially his head.

Jude then noticed that the vibrations that were typical in these circumstances—either from the heavy foot stomping, his father's deep abrasive shouting, or dishware being destroyed—were absent. Either he missed the doors slamming, and the sound of their cars peeling out of the driveway, or he was too involved with the game. They were gone though. And that brought a sense of ease. Each press of the button, watching Mario jump, or throw fireballs, brought small satisfaction. Even just seeing him run across the screen felt like ecstasy.

A flash, followed by what sounded a bit like a sizzling frying pan, hit him from behind. Jude spun around to see a small silhouette and a throne room, like one of those he saw in the old Bible movies his dad

4

watched. It was only visible for a moment, but he caught sight of a woman rushing toward him, armed guards in purple robes with swords in their hands. They looked like something maybe out of Egypt, maybe an Arabic group. The walls looked cloth, like a canvas bag, or a large tent with lanterns perched around the room. Jude had never seen anything like it.

"Barak!" the woman cried, rushing at him. And then she, and the room, disappeared.

Standing behind Jude was a small boy, maybe half his own age. He was very short, even for the age he appeared. His hair was held in intricate, tight braids. Stained purple robes draped over the boy, meeting the dirty sandals on his feet. Dirty everything, Jude noticed.

"Uh," Jude broke the silence. "Excuse me?"

The little boy stood motionless, staring at the TV.

"Hello?" Jude continued. "Are you looking for Sarah?"

Jude's sister had weird friends. Because Jude was older, they all idolized him and always seemed to find ways into his personal space. His parents' arguments usually kept them preoccupied, allowing the children to do whatever they wanted.

Still, the boy remained statuesque; not a muscle moved. Jude wondered if he was a mold.

"Look," Jude said. "You're getting dirt in my room and I don't want to get blamed for that."

Jude paused his game, walked around to the small boy, and put out his hand to shove him back. When he approached, the boy stepped back making Jude jump. It was the first Jude noticed him moving, and therefore alive.

Jude shook his head, furrowing his brow.

"Hey," Jude exclaimed. "You need to get out of my room."

A sound came out of the boy's mouth. It was familiar, but it wasn't a word. Or, at least, it didn't at first sound like a word.

"W-what?" Jude stammered. "Say that again."

5

The boy stared at the screen.

"Dude," Jude started. "I need you out. I don't wanna get blamed fo—"

As his hand connected with the bare skin on the boy's arm, one might have thought Jude was a lightning rod. The boy howled, his free arm whipping around and slamming into Jude's chest, dropping him.

"Holy shit!' Jude shouted as he scurried to get into a crab position, pushing himself a few feet toward the door in the process.

The little boy's arms snagged Jude's pant cuffs and pulled him in. He was far stronger than he appeared. As he got eye level, straddling over Jude with his face mere inches away, he started to ramble. It sounded like gibberish. It seemed like the boy spoke so fast that maybe his words were actually running backward. A few sounded familiar, and Jude realized it was the language he'd heard at Synagogue.

The boy cocked his head to the side, and one of his eyes drifted toward the corner of its socket. A hyena-like smile seeped across his face, and he grabbed Jude's collar, pulling him up.

"What the fuck..." Jude whispered in a breathless tone. "What the fuck..."

Releasing one arm from Jude's collar, the boy placed his hand to his chest and spoke slowly.

"Yeshua..." the boy hissed, as his expression froze in the psychotic grin. "Ye-shu-a."

His eyes returned to center, gesturing back at Jude.

"M-me?" he stammered.

The boy nodded.

"Jude," he replied. "I'm Ju—"

The boy's hand snapped around Jude's head, pulling his face until it was almost pressed against his own. He shrieked as though his lungs were as big as hot air balloons. Somewhere between a hawk and a jet engine, Jude couldn't help but to cry out in response.

Maybe the neighbors would hear.

Maybe the police would come.

However, with all the broken plates and hollering that came out of their house, why would this time be any different?

The boy stopped abruptly, his head cocking to the other side with a loud *pop*. Locking eyes with Jude, his lips curled back to reveal little chiclet teeth the color of cigarette filters, dotted with black spots around the gums. His breath was like rotten milk, hot against Jude's face.

"Yeshua," he grumbled. "Ye-shu-A!" He shook Jude with each syllable.

"Yeshua," Jude replied. "Yeshua. Yeshua."

The boy's arms relaxed around Jude's head, and he lowered him back down toward the floor. Jude felt something wet and warm on the floor as he rolled his back against it. He'd pissed himself.

Now the boy—named Yeshua, Jude had gathered—stood over him and, with a furrowed brow, held out his hand gesturing it was his turn.

Swallowing, Jude stuttered his name.

"J-J-Jude. Jude Scarowsky."

Yeshua's face shifted from focused to excited. One of his eyebrows raised, his mouth agape, he responded back in kind. "Y-Yudah?"

"No," Jude started. "Not 'Yudah.' Jude. Jude."

"Yudah!" Yeshua exclaimed excitedly. "Yudah ish krayot!"

That name struck Jude. Why did it sound so familiar?

Dancing, Yeshua waved his arm up at the wall. Jude heard that sizzling sound again as a flash point burst outward, revealing a dark hole. Jude's eyes widened as he took in the sight. He thought he saw stars, but little else.

Yeshua grabbed Jude and pulled him up. Jude's hands, slipping in the urine beneath him, slid around as he attempted to force himself up. Yeshua was on a rampage; his speech quickened as the words came out so fast that Jude was sure he wouldn't understand him even if he spoke the language.

"What's going on?" Jude demanded. "What is that?"

It reminded him of the movie his mother let him watch, The Black Hole, because she felt he wasn't old enough for Star Wars. Given how the movie ended, he didn't like that Yeshua was pushing him toward the hole that had just opened up in his room.

Jude's urine-soaked hands grabbed at Yeshua's arms.

"Stop!" Jude pleaded. "No, Yeshua, sto—"

Yeshua's arms slipped out from Jude's grip. And with a staccato cackle, his arms snapped forward, shoving Jude. The sensation was like many Jude had experienced during summers at the pool. Older kids at the pool they visited, the ones who called him "kike" and "Christ killer," would shove him when he stood near the edge of water. First was the initial shock of being pushed, the very brief, emancipated feeling of free fall, and then water resistance.

This time, there was no distinct moment between the free fall and the contact with the water. There was no moment between air resistance and water resistance. Instead, it was a sudden sensation of something, other than air, carrying him as his body traversed through the two spaces. Jude wasn't sure what it was, but he held his breath regardless.

Like the pool scenario had reversed, there was a quick transition back to free fall.

"Oh fuck!" he cried. "Shit, shit, shit!"

The ground came up to meet him with little warning, but not with nearly the impact Jude feared. In fact, it almost felt cushioned.

His body rolled with the momentum he gained from falling for a second or two. As he rolled, he noticed the hot, gritty sensation of sand. He couldn't tell if it was the urine he had laid in previously, or the sweat that had already started to pour down his forehead, but he felt moist and dirty with the sand now clinging to him.

Hitting a small recession in the ground, Jude rolled up, and then back down into the hole. Coming to rest on his side, his breath was heavy and ached with each inhale. His heart raced as his breath left him, increasing his anxiety with the worry his heart was going to explode.

Sand covered his face, crevices he normally ignored suddenly ached with the added friction of the burning ruffage. And the heat. How he could do without the heat. He was taunted enough by his classmates for sweating so much when there was tension, or perhaps a presentation due that day. The heat made his sweating a great deal worse and, coupled with his anxiety, much more noticeable and bothersome.

Pushing himself up, the sand that had accumulated in Jude's clothes, his hair, his orifices, and the folds of his skin started to pour back to the earth. Wiping the sweat, littered with grains of sand, from his forehead and eyes, his vision focused enough to be able to make out what was around him: almost nothing. The sky, clearer than he had ever seen it, was spotted like tiny pin pricks through a deep, dark navy sheet. A few yards away was a bright light. Jude squinted to see a silhouette, and his TV.

"Yeshua!" he cried, scaling up the incline on all fours. He hopped to his feet and sprinted toward the light.

"Yeshua, you son of a—" the hole started to close. "No!"

It felt as if knives stabbed at his thighs; a rash had already started to build. Nothing was worth his time, attention, or effort more than reaching the hole.

A child's giddy laugh came from the hole.

"No…" his lungs seared with pain. "Please…"

The sizzling sound the hole made was dwindling, the light became dimmer. Jude was running on the balls of his feet. The laugh, the sizzle, and the light were all dissipating into the darkness.

Hot tears streaked back into his ears. "Please…" came out one last, whimpered cry.

With what felt like his final bit of strength, Jude leapt toward what was left of the opening, missing it by a foot.

With a warm hum, the hole, light, and laugh disappeared.

Jude barely had a moment to lift his head, only to catch a dark, slender figure rise up from the desert sand.

All he could hear was a hiss.

2

"F-f-f-" the word wouldn't come out. "F-f-f-u—"

A hiss, and Jude was startled back into silence.

Mere inches from his face, his eyes were only able to make out small details. However, Jude knew a snake when he saw one. Its head bobbed ever so slightly; its body, wrapped in a loose coil behind it, would twist gently, allowing its head to move in slight gestures toward him.

The snake's tongue flickered out, sometimes slapping itself in the face with gentle strokes. The mouth would open slightly, as if it were smacking its lips, tasting the air around it. Perhaps the urine and sweat made the air taste more appealing. Given the landscape, who knows when the snake had eaten its last meal.

Jude attempted to rise up in slow, intentional moves. The snake's tail quickly whipped from side to side and its jaw opened and closed.

"F-f-f-f-f-u—"

Its head swiveled.

Jude pursed his lips and started inching backward, realizing that standing up would only prepare him to gain distance without getting any space in the process.

The snake's tongue flickered, but it remained in place.

Sand collected in Jude's damp shirt, piling into the folds along the inside. He worried that maybe another living venomous thing might try to crawl in. Or attack him where he was vulnerable. How could he tell? How would he know? When their fangs were already in his body? Jude

11

didn't even know where he was, let alone how the animals native to the region behaved.

A hiss, and Jude jumped back. The snake perked up higher than before, its mouth now gaping. Had it been daytime, and if this were a cartoon, Jude could see a scenario with the sun glinting off the fangs and venom dripping to the ground. And if he were in a cartoon, he could really use a dropped ACME anvil right now. Its head snapped forward, and Jude screeched. He launched himself away from the snake, landing on his back.

"Fuck!" He found his voice. "Fuck! Fuck! Fuck!"

Jude typically avoided swearing, fearing the wrath of his parents if he were ever caught. The "F" word just held all the right sounds and enunciation. And if he were to die right here, would his parents really be so unable to understand his reason for using the word?

Snapping its head twice more, Jude crawled back away from the snake in a panic-stricken fervor.

"Shit!" his vocabulary suddenly expanded. "God dammit!" Being uncensored by parents really permitted him to explore the right curse word for the moment.

"Fuck!"

He heard something like a muted click, and a singing hiss. Jude could make out the tail of the snake whipping back and forth.

"Oh fuck," he whimpered. "Fuck!"

He swore it was slow motion, but the snake appeared to leap toward him. Jude brought his arms up, one covering his face, the other out-stretched as if hoping to catch the snake before it got to him. Instead, he heard shuffling, a *thwack*, ruffling movement, sand being kicked about, and the sound of something, a blade perhaps, being unsheathed. Looking up, Jude saw a figure hunched over, arm up over their head, their back to Jude. The arm slammed down with a slimy gush.

Jude panted, his lips and hands shook. Finally, someone! A person. He could find out where he was, how to get home, and hopefully back to Mario.

"*Abba?*" he heard cried out behind him. Jude whipped his head around to see, coming up from behind a small hill, a woman carrying a lantern and three small boys.

"He-hello?" Jude called. A hand touched his ankle, and Jude jumped, balking in shock.

"Shhhh…" the figure silenced him.

As the light reached them, Jude was finally able to make out the appearance of the figure. It was an older man, perhaps in his fifties or sixties. While not completely gray, there was certainly plenty in his beard. The cloth he wore over his body looked rough, like burlap. There were dark stains covering it. His skin was more olive in tone, and, if Jude had to go off of the stereotypes others used for him, the man might've been Jewish. Or perhaps just Arabic.

"Sir?" Jude asked. "Where… where am I?"

The man's response, though gentle and soothing, was an absolute unintelligible mess to Jude. The man being Arabic seemed much more plausible now.

"Sir," Jude pleaded. "You have to help me." He sat up, clasping his hands together. "I beg you, please!"

The man shook his head, a light smirk on his face.

"English?" Jude said. "Can you…" he turned to the children and woman. "English? Do you understand?"

The man's hands found their way to Jude's shoulders, turning him back toward him. One hand left his shoulder, placed against his own chest, and he calmly said, "Yosef."

Gesturing back at him, Jude remembered this game. So he pointed back at the man.

"Yosef," Jude said, to which the man nodded graciously. His eyes widened and his brow furrowed, turning his head toward Jude, who replied with his own name.

Yosef's head pulled back. His look had gone from hope and ease, to intense interest and excitement. "Yudah?" he asked.

Jude nodded, sighing. "Yes," he surrendered. "Yudah."

Yosef's eyes darted around, looking at Jude, then back at the woman and children, and all around them. He gave a bellowing cry toward the heavens.

"*Eloi! Eloi!*" Words Jude recognized slightly. "My God" was the best understanding he'd had from what precious few moments he'd paid any attention at synagogue. The rest may as well have been in Japanese. From his tone, however, Jude could tell this was a significant moment for the man.

Jude felt other sets of hands placed on him from behind. Some small and fidgety, at least one was of an adult. Calm, intentional.

"*Yosef?*" came a woman's voice.

Jude turned to see the woman just as excited as Yosef had been. The three children, two looking roughly his age, the other a few years younger, were looking at Jude with immense focus.

"Yudah!" Yosef exclaimed, pointing at Jude. The woman gasped; her grip tightened on Jude's shoulders. He felt one of her hands release and heard a shuffle behind him. The woman placed herself in front of him on her knees.

This woman was younger than Yosef by a significant margin. She was perhaps in her mid-twenties to early thirties. A lot of her characteristics matched Yosef's. Stereotypically Jewish, or Arabic, olive skin, and darker black hair. Jude found her pretty, but with a presence very similar to his mother's. At least, not when she was throwing dishes or cursing at his father. Her eyes were as wide as when he first caught sight of her face.

14

"Yudah?" she asked. Jude nodded. Placing her free hand on her chest, she stuttered. "M-Ma-" she chuckled, clearing her throat. "Ma-Mar—"

"Maryam," Yosef finished, placing his arm over her shoulder. He squeezed her tight, and she squealed with excitement, placing her hand over her mouth.

Looking over Jude's shoulder, Maryam waved the boys over to her. The youngest ran over quickly, jumping up and down as he reached his mother. She hugged him and twisted back and forth. With short dark hair, similar scratchy-looking robes, and darker skin, all three children shared the same characteristics as the rest of their family. The older two walked over with purpose, the oldest keeping his arms crossed. Looking at Jude, Maryam pointed at the youngest.

"Shimon," she said, and the young boy giggled.

"Ya'akov," said the older boy, pulling Shimon to stand in front of him.

Jude looked at all of them as they had been presented.

"Yosef," Jude started, gesturing at the patriarch, who nodded in response. "Maryam... Shimon... Ya'akov..." and he came to the last child.

With a devilish grin, the child responded, "Yeshua."

Jude shrieked, catching the others off guard. All jumped at Jude's response, Yosef thrusted himself in front of them with his arms out.

Jude kicked, pushing himself further from the group.

"Yudah!" the patriarch shouted.

Jude stopped, locking his eyes on Yeshua, his chest heaving.

"Go the fuck away," he sobbed. "Just go..."

When Jude looked up at Yosef, he saw he was looking at Maryam. Both had tears streaming down their faces, smiles from ear to ear.

"What... what?" Jude became furious. "What is happening? Where am I?"

Jumping up, he stumbled backward. His heart slammed against his rib cage, hands shaking.

"I want to go home," he shouted. "Now!" Jude pulled his hands back through his hair, sand flitting out with each strand slipping out of his grip.

"This is too much," he cried. "I smell like pee! I'm covered in sweat and sand. A snake almost killed me. *This* prick..." he pointed at Yeshua. "*This* jerk brought me out here and... and..."

Jude dropped to his knees. The tears burned his eyes. "I can't do this," he wailed. "I can't keep feeling like this. I—"

A gentle hand caressed his back. Jude looked up to see Yosef kneeling beside him. Maryam appeared on his other side, her hand stroking his hair. The boys all came into the light. They looked worried. Shimon was sniffling.

Shimon reminded Jude of Sarah, and he reminded himself of what his mother always taught him. Outbursts like that can be scary to younger children who don't know what's going on. They don't understand, so do your best to control those emotions.

Yosef reached into his robe and pulled out a leathery pouch, strings tied around it with a stopper in the top. Uncorking the pouch, he handed it to Jude. Taking the pouch in both hands, Jude brought the opening to his mouth. The first sip brought a bittersweet, yet savory taste to his palate. Spitting the concoction out, choking on the flavor, Yosef hushed him yet again.

"Water?" Jude gurgled out. "Do you have water? Agua? Fuck, I don't know the Hebrew word for water."

Before the tears started streaking down his face again, Yosef shushed him once more, bringing the pouch to Jude's mouth. Dropping his head, Jude took the skin and opted to guzzle the floor-tile flavored beverage. Assuming he was so close to dying anyway, especially with no way to communicate, he may as well die quicker with whatever they were serving him.

Coughing after taking in a large quantity of the fluid, Jude looked up at the family. Their eyes locked on him in amazement. Even Jacob, the more stern-looking older brother, appeared fascinated despite attempts to make himself present as disinterested. Little Shimon bounced on his heels as he fixated on Jude, and Yeshua appeared... different. His features had become much softer and, surprisingly to Jude, he thought he saw some resemblance to himself in Yeshua. More importantly, he looked nothing like the little boy who had tossed him through the hole into this desert land. The tension felt as if it melted off of his chest and shoulders.

"I'm so sorry," Jude moaned, bringing the pouch back to his lips. "I don't know what came over me. I..." He took a large gulp. "I'm so sorry," he whispered.

Jude handed the pouch back to Yosef, who immediately put his hand up, pushing the pouch back toward him. Gesturing at Jude to continue drinking, he sat back and watched in amazement. They sat in a small circle around Jude, Maryam rubbing his back. Yosef started to hum a melody, the boys following along. They swayed back and forth in tempo, eyes closed. Maryam rested her head on Jude's and stroked his hair.

Jude took another deep swig of the fluid, ignoring the putrid taste. Something about it helped him relax. The melody Yosef hummed brought comfort and ease. Jude felt the way that movies about being on the beach made him feel; all those old Elvis Presley films with romance and summer vibes brought a very care-free, relaxing tone to his house. And this felt so much the same.

Whether it was the actual sand beneath him, the melodies being sung, or the care provided for him by this family of strangers, Jude finally started to feel what he thought was missing. Acceptance. Attention. Care. Love.

The pouch became lighter and lighter as the man continued to sing. Maryam kissed the top of Jude's head periodically and whispered something he couldn't understand to him. He imagined she was telling him all would be well. He was protected now, and he would be safe from those terrible feelings.

Jude started to feel drowsy. He was finding it more and more difficult to bring the pouch opening to his mouth, or even to sit up. Maryam giggled a few times as he started to fall backward. She missed him and he chuckled as he hit the sand behind him. Shimon laughed like a crazy man as it happened, and his laugh made everyone laugh.

"This is what it should be like," Jude slurred to the others. "This is how family should be." He drained the remaining few gulps into his mouth, wiping it dry with his free hand. "I want to be a part of this family," he said.

Whether they understood him or not, they all smiled at him. Maryam hugged him close.

Jude's eyes flickered.

"I don't remember the last time my mom hugged me," he said.

A tear fell down his cheek, and he started to snore.

3

Jude awoke to a thin slit of light streaked directly across his eyes. The sun appeared to have become ever more luminous since he had last seen daylight. His head was heavy, like he had contracted the flu, and the room spun as he tried to push himself up.

Licking his lips, Jude tasted mud. Had he been sleeping on the ground? Looking around, he noticed he was in a small hut made from loosely placed stones and piles of mud and straw. The sun had burst in through one of the windows that had a thin veil over the opening. It felt like he had awoken under water. From how his eyes felt, he could have come to immersed in bleach. Rubbing his eyes, he spat out chunks of dirt and mud. His hands, covered in dust, only made the pain in his eyes worse as he massaged more filth into them. Standing up, he cringed as tears cleared away the dirt.

Stumbling as he stood, Jude felt a breeze stroking against the skin of his legs, up his thigh, and against his genitals. Blinking furiously, he looked down to discover he was in a tunic type of uniform. It may have originally been an off-white color, but it was stained with brown and tan patches. His clothing was nowhere in sight.

All the memories came flooding back. The bizarre portal that the first Yeshua pushed him through. Encountering the snake in the middle of the desert. And the family he encountered, with the other Yeshua. For some reason, this was the straw that broke the camel's back for Jude.

"I want to go home…" Jude wept, his face contorted into a grimace. Pulling the collar of his tunic up, he wiped his eyes and buried his face in his hands. "I want to go home," came an airy whine from Jude.

"*Yudah?*" came a soft, feminine voice from behind him. Jude looked up to see two girls, only a few years older than he, standing in the doorway to the hut. Their black hair, frizzy and wildly wrapped over their shoulders, looked like they had rubbed inflated balloons over their heads before meeting with him. They both were adorned in similar tunics with similar stains across them. Their faces, striped with dirt, read with sadness and concern. One of them, the youngest of the two, softly asked Jude something. Furrowing his brow, he shook his head.

"What?" Jude whimpered.

The younger girl stated something that sounded similar to what she had asked before, but Jude still was lost. "I don't understand," he muttered. "I'm sorry, I…" he burst into tears, shoving his face back in his hands and continued, "I can't understand a god damn thing," he groaned.

Two hands caressed his back. He felt a head rest against the top of his.

"Shhhhh…" came a soothing hush from one of the girls. They whispered to him. Incomprehensible, but still relaxing. It reminded him of the talks his mother had with him after she and his father fought. As if to tell him this was a nightmare, but everything would be alright. Tears flowed harder, but perhaps they did because of the ease and reassurance he received from their gesture.

The moment was broken up with the sound of a soothing, warm, male voice.

"Yehudit… Rahel," came the gentle call.

All three turned to find Yosef standing before the door. He smiled, but he had wet streaks along the front of his face. His lip quivered as he watched them.

"Abba?" asked the older girl. Yosef nodded at her and gestured outside. Lowering their heads, the girls both gave Jude one last circular rub on his back and walked with purpose out of the hut.

Yosef walked over and, kneeling in front of Jude, put his arms around him. His hug was warm, snug, and comforting. Jude became overwhelmed. Not even his own father hugged him and this man, who he had almost no connection to, embraced him like family.

"Yudah," sobbed Yosef pulling away from him. Stopping himself before he spoke, Yosef looked to the upper right corner of his eyes. Gesturing with his hand like he was gripping a deck of cards, he tapped his lips with the tips of his fingers. Without a moment's hesitation, Jude frantically nodded.

"Please," Jude sobbed. "Please, I'm so hungry."

Yosef walked out of the hut, a fire in his step. As he exited, one of the boys entered.

"Yeshua?" asked Jude.

The boy turned, looked Jude up and down and giggled. "Ta'oma," he replied, a smile spreading from ear to ear.

"I don't understand," Jude replied. "I... I don't speak your language."

Yosef emerged from the doorway, a thin piece of bread with an oily drizzle running down the face of it in his hand. Looking back and forth between them, he cocked his head and his eyes narrowed as they locked on his son. The boy smiled up at his father, and they both chuckled as Yosef handed Jude the bread. Taking the bread, Jude wolfed it down, feeling as if he'd not eaten in days. Yosef knelt between them, placing his hand on his son's back.

"Yudah," he said, gesturing at the other boy. "Ta'oma."

Jude placed his hand over his mouth, struggling to swallow. "I don't know what that means," he said, feeling wet pieces of food hit his palm. "Does Yeshua..."

Yosef's hand went up in front of Jude's face. Shaking his head, he pointed back at the boy.

"Ta'oma," Yosef stated again.

"I don't…" Jude started to say. The other boy grabbed him by the collar and dragged him to the doorway. With a gentle push out the door, the boy pointed out. There, a few yards from where they stood, Yeshua played in a puddle.

Jude blinked, wiped the backs of his hands on his tunic, and rubbed his eyes. Turning around, he saw Yosef come out into the sunlight with a wide grin. Placing his arm around the boy, they both gave a nasally chuckle.

Jude turned back, pointing at the boy in the puddle. "Yeshua?" he asked, looking back at the pair.

Yosef nodded. Pointing back at the other boy, he asked, "Ta'oma?" The boy raised his arms triumphantly, jumping up and down. He babbled to Yosef in their native tongue, sounding possessed and nonsensical. Yosef gave out a hearty laugh and patted Ta'oma on the head.

"Twins!" Jude declared.

As Jude loudly announced his epiphany, a loud warbling came from where Yeshua was sitting, accompanied by the sound of light splashing. Yeshua appeared to struggle with something, and then a bird flew up and away from the boy.

Glancing over his shoulder, Yeshua shot daggers at Jude.

"Yeshua!" called Yosef, marching toward him. Ta'oma and Jude followed close behind.

Wagging his finger at Yeshua, Yosef bent over as he came close to him and spoke to him in a stern voice. Whatever it was, Jude thought Yeshua had done something terrible.

Peering into the hole, Jude saw a large puddle of water surrounded by several small mounds of mud. Twelve in total. Was Yeshua planning on burying the bird? Hitting it with the little mud balls?

As Yosef lectured Yeshua, the boy reached into the puddle without taking his eyes away from his father. Cupping his hand, he took a small amount of the opaque water and drizzled it over one of the mounds of mud.

And it started to move.

Jude's eyes widened; his jaw slacked. The movement morphed into a shake, and brown water flecks arched up and away from the small ball to reveal a bird.

"Yeshua!" exclaimed Yosef.

Without losing eye contact, Yeshua reached back into the puddle and drizzled the water over several of the mud balls. Each one reacted as the first: light movement, shaking, and the emergence of birds. Sparrows.

Jude lunged forward and grabbed one of the balls of mud, squishing it gently in his hand. In his mind he saw these sparrows all trapped in a thick layer of mud, unable to break free until the water was applied. Yet there was no movement in response. Jude sunk a finger into the mud, but it cleared through to the other side unimpeded.

Yeshua reached up, looking at Jude with contempt, and snatched the mud ball out of his hand. Rolling it back into its original shape, he placed it gently in its original position.

"Yeshua!" shouted Yosef. "Shabbat!"

The Sabbath, Jude realized. He was lecturing Yeshua about doing work on the Sabbath.

Yeshua, with a smirk on his face, reached back into the water, and drizzled it across the remaining balls of mud. As before, a quiver turned into a convulsion, mud spraying away, and the revelation of small sparrows, even from the mound that Jude had grasped.

"What the fuck..." Jude whispered.

"*Yosef!*" called a man's voice from behind them. All turned to witness a man, roughly Yosef's age and in similar dress, marching toward them. Two small boys were marching proudly behind him, wicked smiles on their dirt-coated faces. They looked to be around the same age as Yeshua and Ta'oma.

Before reaching what Jude assumed to be a comfortable range for a personal discussion, the man launched into an angry rant in their language. Pointing at Yeshua, the word "Shabbat" was shouted a few times. Yosef stood his ground, his chest thrust out, arms crossed. Closing his eyes and shaking his head, he made several calm attempts to speak to the man who only responded in panicked shrieks.

Yosef stood unflinching. Jude's chest tightened; a cold sweat formed on his brow. His arms burned as he noticed they had tensed up. A swig from Yosef's pouch would've been welcomed.

Jude turned as another sound caught his attention. Mocking, sing-song-like chants came from higher pitched voices. The two boys were pointing at Yeshua and Ta'oma, dancing and making faces at them. Ta'oma sneered at them, his fists balled up and white-knuckled. Yeshua gazed up at them with a blank stare.

While one of the children continued his taunts, the other took notice of Yeshua's laissez faire response. His forehead wrinkled as his brows folded inward. The corners of his mouth pinched downward, exposing his yellow and black tainted teeth.

Screams ejaculated from the boy, spittle flying with each over-articulated consonant of his tirade. His arms waved as if conducting the violent climax of an orchestral movement, causing his companion to flinch. Raising his arm to protect his face, the other child's eyes filled with concern and curiosity.

Jude jumped back with his arms folding in over his chest. His heart rate exploded, creating a pressure in his chest that reminded him of when older boys at school sat on his chest while berating him. Breathing became an Olympic event, becoming harder and harder to take in with each abrasive screech that flew from the boy's mouth.

All the while, Yeshua remained unmoved.

The boy became enraged. As his rant sounded like it was closing, he raised one leg in a sudden jerk and slammed it down on top of two of the sparrows. The sound of light, muffled pops shot up, like he had stepped on a roll of bubble wrap. All the other sparrows had flown off in a cacophony of tweets and fluttering wings.

Yeshua peered down at the boy's foot as a dark, syrupy liquid seeped out and trickled down to the puddle. Yeshua's face turned up, having turned a pale green. His eyes rolled back into his head; a faint light emanated from the edges. Lurching upwards, Yeshua's arms rose, palms up, gesturing toward the boy. Shrieks, with a touch of discernible words, rocketed from Yeshua's spasming jaw.

A choking gurgle spurted out of the boy's mouth. Jerking backward, arching his spine, he slammed his head against the ground. Connecting with a soccer ball sized rock, a sound like a monstrous egg being cracked startled the group. A foamy, gelatinous mix that resembled tomato soup and pink Styrofoam stuck out from the side of the boy's skull. Shaking as he lay on his side, a feces stench, a sewer, wafted up from the convulsing boy. Foam was flowing down his face, out the corners of his mouth. Steam started to rise from the blood draining out of the boy's head.

Snapping his attention toward Yeshua, Jude furrowed his brow as he watched him turn his hands. A wicked smile melted across his face. A crackling noise, a campfire, wet the busy soundscape. Returning his gaze to the boy, the blood that had gushed from the boy's head now started to bubble and rise in a red mist. His skin wrinkled, wrapping tightly around his frame.

A howl exploded from behind them. The child's father ran over and picked up the boy. His once sandy skin darkened to a brown, leathery, beef jerky hide. Remnants of his life force sweeping up into a cloud of red before dissipating into thin air. His father cried; his tears brought a distinct *tap, tap* sound as they fell against the face of his son.

The boy's empty sockets stared up at the weeping man. Baring teeth, the man's lips curled inward, cracked and exposing part of his gums.

Gasping for air, the boy's father hollered at the corpse in his hands. Stroking his head, clumps of hair floated from his plastic skull to the packed sands below. His eyes widened, conscious of the damage he'd caused his already decimated creation.

The weeping man placed the boy's body in the sand like he was a frail antique. Growling, he pushed himself upward and glared at Jude and the brothers. His hand raised, a wavering finger extended as if a blade.

"Yeshua!" the man screamed, startling the group. The dead boy's brother took that opportunity to bolt from the scene. Jumping up, his feet seemed to work faster than his body was prepared for. Face planting several times in his attempt to allude his father's rage, he ended up leaning sideways and elbowed Yeshua in the chest in the process.

An animalistic howl erupted from Yeshua as the other boy stopped, mid-motion, with no warning. Like watching a home video, the boy seemed to be stuck on pause. A purple hue shone from around his body.

"Lo!" yelped the father. "Lo! Lo! Lo!" He sounded like the Hasidic fathers yelling for their child to stop when they had gone to visit Jude's grandparents in Brooklyn.

Yeshua hollered another spattering of Hebrew, and the boy started to shrivel. The same red mist pooled out in a swarm of hissing and crackling. The crackling became louder pops, which then evolved into snaps. Like large tree branches breaking free, the sound was mixed with light gushing and fabric tearing. What once was a boy, rolled up into a basketball sized spheroid. Bones with dried blood stains protruded from the mess, small flaps of flesh, more the texture of jerky, curled into small brown strips.

Torn from the scene, Jude's attention snapped backward as shrieks of fury and a stampede raced toward them. The dead boy's father lunged at them, tears flooding his cheeks. His face a dark amber color, his eyes enraged.

Jude's heart raced as he leapt forward, his calf muscles snapped like whips. His primal instinct took over; protect your tribe. Protect your flock.

As he darted forward, Jude pivoted in front of Yeshua, facing him with his arms outstretched. Without warning, there was a sudden calm. Jude felt something new. It was strange yet soothing.

Calm.

An arm glided under his own; a soft, warm palm flattened itself against his shoulder blade. Pulling back, Jude looked up to see Yeshua smiling at him with contented eyes. Looking over his shoulder, Jude discovered they were no longer in the small village preparing for the rage of the boys' grieving father. Instead, he found they were standing in a room with a glass ceiling. The sky that peaked down on them was a murky orange-red color. Taking a step backward, Jude's feet felt a hard, smooth surface. Looking down, he discovered the floor was as transparent as the ceiling. Below were clouds, teetering on the edge between red and brown. Lightning cracked through, like the timed Christmas lights Jude used to see on his street during the winter holiday season. There appeared to be a new burst of lightning every few seconds.

The sound of an older man clearing his throat made Jude and Yeshua snap their heads toward one end of the room. In a large golden throne sat a green, white, and black splotchy mess of a man. With red hair that melted into straps adorning the sides of his face and under his chin, a dark scar ran down across his neck. A golden crown of leaves sat around his skull. Six seats to either side of him sat various men in military garb, business suits, and tunics. All eyes rested on them.

A smirk ran across the face of the man in the throne, and he raised his hand with a tense thumb up.

"My brother," came a whisper from Yeshua in clear English.

Jude whipped his head back around at Yeshua who was already pulling him in for a tight embrace.

"Wait!" cried Jude.

He tried to pull away, only to jump when he heard a familiar voice screaming. Twisting like a cork screw, he saw the boys' father running at them. With no time to process the how, Jude dashed back toward the hut. His legs felt taught as a bow, his heart jackhammering against his sternum. Breathing felt like inhaling hot coals.

"Yudah!" cried Yeshua.

Jude peered over his shoulder, and he dug his heels into the beaten path.

The man stood motionless. Not just motionless, but frozen mid-stride. Mere inches from Yeshua, with his hand raised, smiling back at Jude, who furrowed his brow, wiping sweat from his eyes.

"See," spoke Yeshua, "and believe."

"Yeshua!" called Yosef.

Yeshua turned and looked at his father, who had a proud smile on his face. Closing his eyes, and placing his hands behind his back, he nodded.

Yeshua's fingers bent at the tips, and a searing sizzle broke the silence. With a wet *bang*, filth erupted from the man's eyes. Tumbling into a haggard mess, the man erupted with screeches of agony. He placed his hands over his eyes, only to rip them off. Dark red, boiling blisters appeared on his hands. Bubbles appeared around the corners of his eyes as he cried.

In the distance, several more cries of fear and pain rocketed out of other huts. People came running out their doors, blood pouring from their eye sockets. A few on their knees, others stumbled over themselves or other obstacles lying outside their homes. Steam and sludge fell from their faces.

"Holy shit!" cried Jude. Hot tears started to flow down his face and he fell onto his back. "Oh shit, oh shit, oh shit..."

Too afraid to touch his face, Jude's breathing became rapid and painful. He felt like Atlas had dropped the world on his chest. His legs shook, violent gasps for air mixed with strained sobs gurgled out of his mouth as he drooled over himself.

"Oh God, oh God…" he cried. Speech became more and more garbled and indecipherable.

A face leaned in, blocking out the sun. As Jude's eyes focused on the face, he saw Yeshua.

"My brother…" Yeshua whispered again.

"NO!" Jude hollered into Yeshua's face. Jude was racing backward in a crab walk, never taking his eyes off Yeshua's smiling face. Jude's hands slipped and scraped over the tops of rocks, sand wedged deep into the cuts. Whimpers slipped through his gritted teeth as he focused on putting more space between himself and Yeshua.

Two sets of arms reached around Jude and pulled him close against two soft, warm bodies. He yelped, snapping his head up and down to keep the subject of his fear within his sight. It was the girls, Yehudit and Rahel. Their faces filled with concern, they stroked Jude's head and let out soft shushes to ease him. One caressed his chest, the other began to hum a gentle, simple song.

Jude's heart felt like it was boxing the girls' hands through his chest. Each muscle quaked, his feet moving as if trying to find the ground to run. As the melody crept through the girls' lips, his heart rate slowed, his body cooled, and his feet came to rest. Choking through tears, snot, and the sand in his mouth, he peered down toward where Yeshua was standing.

Yosef, Ya'akov, Shimon, and Ta'oma all were knelt around Yeshua. All with eyes closed, all in synchronized chant. What they said was lost under the screams of the others, clutching at their eyes, dark red molasses running between their fingers, pooling at their feet.

As the panic crept back into Jude's chest, sweat collecting along his brow, another melody pierced through the air. This song he recognized.

"*I once was lost, but now am found…*"

Jude looked up to see Yeshua lifting off the ground.

"…was blind, but now I see…"

4

All the boys sat in a circle surrounding an older man, wearing a striped robe that reached his ankles and a red belt ornamented with sparkling jewels. Small tassels hung from the edges of his sleeves. He was adorned with a turban-style hat, and he had a long, scraggly, salt-and-pepper-colored beard. Yosef had introduced him as Zacchaeus. Walking in a slow cautious circle, he examined each boy. A stern, disciplined look etched into his face as he paced. Shimon made faces at Zacchaeus as his back was presented to him. Stopping with a sharp, heavy stomp, the man's face looked to a gap between Ta'oma and Ya'akov. Jude sat several feet away, gripping his knees and shivering with anxiety.

"Yudah," called Zacchaeus, gesturing to the open gap.

Jude shook his head.

"Yu. Dah," his tone became authoritative and forceful.

Jude felt a gentle brush on his back. Looking up, the warm smile of Yosef greeted him. He gestured, with a nod, toward the circle, and helped Jude up onto his feet. Guiding him with both hands, Yosef walked with Jude to the circle. As he sat, Yosef ruffled his hair and kissed the top of Jude's head.

Each gesture that these adults, Yosef and Maryam, made toward Jude gave him something he felt he had been starving for, like eating a full meal after fasting for weeks. It made him feel energized, like he could fight on against whatever was holding him back. As he watched Yosef walk back into their hut, Jude heard Zacchaeus' feet shuffle through the dirt once again. His path changed.

Zacchaeus approached Shimon and kicked a small rock at the child. It ricocheted off Shimon's shoulder and landed in Ya'akov's lap. Shimon rubbed his arm, frowning up at the old man as he passed between the two boys.

Clearing his throat, Zacchaeus took a deep breath and blurted out, "Aleph!"

Each of the boys scrambled to scrawl with their index fingers into the dirt. Jude sat for a moment, furrowing his brow. It was so familiar. Where had he heard that before?

Yeshua was the only other one who didn't respond to the command. Instead, a sly grin was painted across his face and a warm, soft chuckle escaped through his nostrils.

A rock slapped Jude in the chest, making him jump and shriek.

"Aleph!" Zacchaeus hollered at him. "Aleph! Aleph! Aleph!"

Looking down at the dirt in front of the other boys, Jude saw a similar pattern of calligraphy drawn by each of them. It was the first letter of the Hebrew alphabet.

In a panic, muttering to himself, Jude hunched over and scrawled what he could remember from his short time learning the Hebrew alphabet. It looked similar to the others. He hoped that the malleability of the dirt would provide an adequate excuse for how messy it looked.

Yeshua still had nothing in front of him.

"Yeshua!" hollered Zacchaeus. "Aleph!"

Yeshua stifled a laugh, covering his mouth. Zacchaeus' face contorted into an angry grimace. "Yeshua!" he shouted again.

With shoulders quaking as he fought harder to stay silent, Yeshua's face grew crimson and his eyelids squeezed tightly. Tears trickled down the creases around his mouth.

"*Yeshua?*" came a deep, commanding call from behind where Jude sat. All the boys turned and looked to see Yosef standing over several piles of wood. With his arms crossed, and a stone in hand, his head slowly tilted forward. His eyes gazed through the tops of his eyelids at Yeshua.

Jude looked back at the boy, his face covered in his hands, moisture trickling between his fingers and down his knuckles. Yeshua took a deep breath, closed his eyes, and removed his hands to reveal a snarky smile. "Zacchaeus?" he asked.

The teacher's eyes narrowed. His brow seemed to tighten and strain across his forehead. Jude swore he saw a throbbing vein in his neck. Zacchaeus grunted at Yeshua. Jude could understand little of what was exchanged between them, but he heard "aleph" and "bet," the second letter of the Hebrew alphabet, a number of times between them.

Zacchaeus, while initially annoyed, started to appear more relaxed in his face. The fury disappeared and was replaced with awe. As Yeshua continued, tears started to drizzle down Zacchaeus' face and become lost in his beard.

What could have possibly been so important about the first two letters of the alphabet that had caused this stern teacher to become reverential toward such a devious child? Jude wondered.

When Yeshua finished, the other boys pursed their lips. Shimon bounced in his seat; gritting his teeth with an excited smile, he tugged on Ya'akov's arm.

Zacchaeus' stammered, struggling to speak and catch his breath at the same time. "Yosef!" he bellowed, whipping around.

Yosef, who was about to hammer down on his project, slipped and split the wooden plank he was working on in half. He dropped the stone and dragged his fingers through his hair, groaning through a strained neck.

"Yosef!" Zacchaeus called again.

Yosef shot upward, like lightning had struck him, shouting as he did. He whipped around, a vivid tempest in his eyes. It looked as if his teeth may crack under the pressure in his jaw.

Both men shouted at one another—Yosef with fire and brimstone, Zacchaeus with enraptured fear. Yosef would stop, mid rant, long enough to catch a word or two of the teacher's persistent rambling. Yosef would repeat back a word or two, only to sound more exasperated.

With a gurgle, and a twitch, Zacchaeus arched his back and froze.

"Oooooooh…" Shimon sang.

Jude turned his head slowly to find Yeshua with his hand raised in a familiar gesture. In a relaxed hold, his index and middle finger raised together, pinky and ring drooped down over his palm. His thumb stood at attention. And his eyes glazed over with a cloudy yellowish-white color that seemed to glow like candles in a distant window.

"Fuck," Jude muttered as his feet shot him away from the circle.

Yeshua's head dragged to the side, as if sliding down a pillow. His mouth moved like he was singing, in a rhythmic twitch.

Several loud snaps caught the boys' attention, their heads tossed back in the direction of the sound. Zacchaeus appeared bent in half, backward. With a wet burp sound, the top half of his torso and his lower legs snapped in opposite directions. Blood rocketed out of his mouth and his skin became a dark, almost purple, color as it started to shrivel and sizzle.

After another twitch and a series of snaps, Zacchaeus' eyes burst, a crimson jelly drenching Ta'oma. Ta'oma flopped onto his belly, retching onto the ground behind him. Shimon clapped his hands as Ya'akov pulled him away from the mess.

Jude watched as the teacher continued to crack, gush, fizzle, and steam. In a slow, agonizing display, Zacchaeus started to form into a ball. His deep, festering eye sockets appeared to make a connection with Jude. Out of his mouth came a gurgled, "*Shhhhhhhatan…*"

With a final violent *pop*, Zacchaeus' face imploded into the sputtering mess that lay before them. Jude's jaw quivered. His stomach was overcome with abrupt contractions. Rolling over, he spewed greenish-yellow bile onto the ground before him.

34

Giggling started to break the quiet moaning and gleeful clapping coming from the brothers. A hand gave a gentle tug on Jude's shoulder, and he rolled to find Yeshua standing over him. An innocent smirk rained down to greet Jude, who could only quiver in response.

"Please don't hurt me," Jude pleaded in a whisper.

In response, Yeshua started to hum a tune. It was another one Jude had heard before. Classmates had sung it—the ones who teased him and called him "Jew" on the playground.

"Yeshua!" called Yosef. Jude and Yeshua both looked over at Yosef, gesturing down at the broken wooden plank at his feet.

Without stopping his song, Yeshua ran over to Yosef. Picking up one of the broken ends, Yeshua held it in both hands and simply pulled. As elastic as a piece of silly putty, the plank stretched out to the length it had been before. Yosef patted him on the back as Yeshua handed him the board.

Jude, sure that he had hallucinated it, or that he was dreaming, lay on his side and quaked. Foam started to accumulate at the corner of his mouth. Tears fell without effort down his face.

Ta'oma, dragging his feet, sauntered over and flopped down next to Jude. He took a large swig from the wine skin in his hand, swished it in his mouth, and swallowed with a loud gulp. He guided the skin over to Jude's lips, and with eager, convulsing hands, he gripped the wine skin and guzzled the contents. Ta'oma's hand rubbed Jude's back as Yeshua came dancing back over, still humming the song from before.

As his melody reached the end of its repetitive phrase, Yeshua swung his leg back and gave an enthusiastic kick at the balled-up teacher on the ground. Blood sprayed from the collision of foot and man, like a wet pool ball, and the contorted corpse flew off down the beaten path. Jude hardly noticing his own face, now freckled with plasma, pulled his lips away from the wine skin.

He remembered the song.

As Ta'oma took the skin from Jude's hands, Jude sang just over a whisper.

"This is the day that the Lord has made, let us be glad and rejoice..."

5

Biting the tips of his fingers, Jude stared out the window at the brothers as they laughed and shoved one another. Playing a game of keep-away, they held a small piece of unleavened bread over Shimon's head.

"Jesus…" Jude whispered. "Jesus… Jesus…"

A soft, feminine voice behind him called, clearing her throat. Jude jumped, turning so his back was against the wall, his arms folding across his chest. Yehudit and Rahel stood, side by side, holding some of the bread and a wine skin. Jude, spotting the wine skin, lunged forward.

Both girls recoiled and Jude froze. Realizing how he may have looked to them, he pressed himself back up against the wall.

"I'm… I'm sorry," Jude whispered. He lowered his head as his vision became blurry with tears.

Two sets of feet approached him, and the bread was held under his face. Already drizzled with a thin trace of oil. Jude stared for a moment at the bread. He wished for a hamburger. Grilled cheese. Chicken noodle soup. Anything more than this paltry sustenance they ate ad nauseam. With a shaky sigh, Jude took one of his arms off his chest and reached for the bread.

"Thank—" he stopped. Closing his eyes, tears dripped from his eyelashes. He knew, if he dug deep enough into his memory from his Hebrew lectures, he could remember the word he was searching for.

After a moment, he cleared his throat.

"Todah, Rahel…"

"Yehudit," she replied.

Glancing up, Jude's eyes connected with the girl's wide, dark-brown eyes. A small, innocent smile spread across her face.

"Yehudit," she repeated.

"T-todah…" Jude said again. "Yehudit."

Yehudit released the bread as Jude slowly brought it to his face. Closing his eyes, he thought of pizza as his teeth sank into the soft aerated dough. The hint of oil made him remember all the dinners his father had taken him and his mother out to, and how he used to focus on eating the bread. While waiting for their main course to arrive, Jude ate the bread dipped in oil and parmesan to distract from the passive-aggressive arguments his parents engaged in. Now, he felt, he could enjoy the bread without needing the escape.

Jude still missed home. And his video games.

Stuffing the remainder into his mouth, Jude reached for the wine skin. Rahel, with a sorrowful smile, placed it in his outstretched hand. Jude immediately brought the container to his lips, mindful to take it slow. He took in a light amount to wash down the dry crumbs that stuck in his throat. The bitter, stinging taste of the liquid burned the back of his gullet as it loosened the food and slid down to his belly. That sting had become so familiar, and he wanted more.

Closing his eyes, and taking a deep breath, Jude fought the urge to down the rest of the container. Once he'd overheard his father fighting with his mother about how children had no sense of self-control after Jude spent the entire weekend in his room playing video games. His parents, with a heavier push from his father, were fanatical about keeping up appearances. Jude never pointed out to his father that he stayed the entire weekend in his room because of how heated the arguments got, fearful he may have to report something he had witnessed his father had done to his mother. It was better they thought he was playing video games than knowing he was crying under his blankets. It was then that he started to retreat into his games.

"Todah, Rahel," Jude gasped, finally forcing a look of appreciation rather than exasperation. Bringing the wine skin back to his lips, he took several more large gulps, embracing the sharp sting of the bitter wine.

Shaking his head, eyes clenched, Jude knew the girls were reaching out for the wine. He had already raised concern by drinking more than he should have on two separate occasions. "Rahel..." he started. "Rahel... Rachel?"

Opening his eyes, both girls had raised eyebrows, Yehudit looking back and forth between Jude and Rahel. Jude pointed at Rahel with his free hand, taking another swig from the wine skin.

"Abrit, Rahel," Jude said. "English, Rachel."

Looking at Yehudit, Jude followed with, "Abrit, Yehudit," she smiled as his hand extended toward her. "English... Judith."

Jude and Yehudit continued this game, referring to Shimon and Ya'akov as Simon and James. Looking out the window, Jude pointed toward the twins and asked, "Yeshua? Ta'oma?"

The girls crept up to the window, peering out. Jude took another deep swig from the wine skin.

Shimon sat atop Ya'akov's shoulders as one of the twins attempted to grab the piece of bread from the young boy's hand. Giggles, shouts, and dust scattered through the air. Another one of the twins sat, eating his bread and guarding his face from the dirt with a sneer. Yehudit pointed at the twin that was sitting.

"Ta'oma," she said,

"Thomas," Jude replied. "English, Thomas."

"Yeshua," said Rahel, pointing at the other.

A wave of fear suddenly spread over Jude's face.

"J-J-" he took another gulp of wine. "Jesus Christ."

Both girls looked at Jude, worry prominent in their faces. Without making eye contact, Jude sighed.

"You wouldn't understand..." he started.

"Christos?" asked Yehudit.

Jude looked up at them, shocked to hear, not only a non-Hebrew word from them, but one he recognized.

"Yes…" Jude said, surprised. His heart started to race.

"Mashiach…" said Rahel.

That word Jude recognized, without question.

The sounds from outside grew louder, as if someone turned up a volume knob on a stereo with caution. Peering between the girls, several other children had joined the brothers. Ta'oma had made his way further back to continue his private picnic.

"Mashiach," Yehudit repeated, with a tone of finality.

"Messiah," Jude replied.

From the front door, Maryam entered, dragging young Shimon in behind her. He was crying, clutching his forearm, which had a slight trickle of blood. With a contented smile, Maryam made a repetitive *tsk* sound through her teeth.

"Shimon, Shimon, Shimon," she cooed.

The little boy huffed and whined as he was sat on the floor across from Jude and the girls. Removing Shimon's hand from his arm, Maryam spit on the wound and rubbed it into the scrape. Taking his small tunic, she wrapped it around his arm and returned his hand to the wound, pressing tightly.

"Mary…" Jude whispered. His mind brought him back to the number of times he heard his parents say things like "Holy Mary, Mother of God," or "Jesus, Mary, and…"

"Yosef!" Maryam called.

A loud banging sound, that was so often in the background Jude never noticed it until now, had stopped. It was replaced by heavy footsteps along gravel and fatigued breathing. Through the doorway emerged Yosef, drenched in sweat, marked with dried mud and sand that glistened from the sun's reflection off his skin.

"Abba," came a prideful pronouncement from the girls. They bounded over to him as he hugged them with gratitude, kissing the tops of their heads.

"Joseph," Jude belched out. His hand clasped over his mouth as all eyes darted toward him.

Yosef smiled, rubbing the backs of his daughters. Releasing them, he walked over toward Jude. His hands on Jude's shoulders, a gentle lean turned it into a hug, pulling Jude into Yosef's chest. Jude, in reflex, wrapped his arms around Yosef.

"Yudah," Yosef hummed. Pulling away from him, and resting on one knee, Yosef placed his hand on his own chest and said, "Abba."

Jude looked down at his feet. He felt as conflicted as when he'd hid himself in his room. Coupled with the abject horror of realizing, not only might he never return home, but now he was being asked to join the family of the most influential figure in history. And that figure was a monster.

Leaning in closer to Jude, Yosef repeated himself.

"Abba."

Placing a gentle hand on Jude's chest, Jude clasped his free hand over Yosef's.

"Ben," Yosef started. "Yudah ben Yosef."

"Jude, son of Joseph," Jude whispered. "Yudah…"

He stopped, choking back tears. Yosef took his other hand and guided the wine skin, still in Jude's hand, up to his mouth. With hands shaking, Jude guzzled another gulp down his throat. After a breath, he let out a cathartic sigh. The relief that came with the drink hit him at last, and the tension in his muscles dissipated.

"Yudah ben Yosef," he smiled. Hot tears fell down his cheeks as a smile formed on his face. Yosef bit his bottom lip as his eyes welled up. Pulling Jude in for a hug, and Jude hugging back, he could feel Yosef's tears flow down along the back of his neck.

Jude looked up to see Maryam and the girls suppressing sobs, wet streaks on their faces. They hugged Shimon who gave a silent applause, grinning so wide it looked as if his teeth might fall out. In what felt like a rarity, Jude smiled. This felt like love, like acceptance. He had done something that brought joy to others instead of a shouting contest.

This felt like where he belonged.

With a heavy stomp, all looked up and toward the doorway. Ya'akov was panting, fear in his eyes. "Abba!" he hollered.

Yosef, in one fluid motion, rose and leapt out the door. Followed by the girls, Maryam carried Shimon, and Jude jogged behind them. He finished what was in the skin and tossed it at the ground as he ran out the door.

A small group of boys formed a circle in front of another hut. There was weeping and excited chatter as several other people came close to the huddle. Ya'akov looked back at Yosef and pointed toward the group, panic still emanating from his eyes.

Yosef's pace slowed the closer he got. Jude saw the tension in his stance ease into disappointment, regret. Patting Ya'akov on the shoulder, he continued toward the boys making a gentle call as he approached.

Each boy, turning as Yosef spoke, looked horrified. Their eyes moist and red, snot running into their mouths. Some sniveling and bawling uncontrollably as they looked into their circle. Yosef pulled each from the circle with a gentle urgency Jude recognized from the many manic episodes he had shared with him. Guiding them to other adults or older children approaching the scene, Yosef had all the appearance of an usher at a funeral.

Jude staggered past Maryam and Shimon, whose small voice whispered soft, considerate calls of "*Em!*"

Mom!

Focusing on walking, Jude felt the heaviness in the air. As if the very atmosphere had become depressive and suicidal, and the weight bore down on all. It was too much for anyone there. Even the men were posturing as if they possessed stone-cold, unfeeling hearts.

Jude recognized those looks. When his mother threatened to file for sole custody of him and his sister, his father always stood upright and, with a chilling calm, left the room with a firm, "*Fine.*" But his hands shook in clenched fists at his side. His hypnotic blue eyes shimmered with a coating of fresh tears. The corners of his mouth twitched; his bottom lip quivered in ever the slightest way.

Jude brushed past Yehudit and Rahel, and one of them grabbed at his hand. Raising it in a feigned wave, he slowly stumbled past more onlookers. Now he saw what they were gathered around.

A woman, roughly Maryam's age, held a child in her arms. His head was bloodied, neck bent at an impossible angle; his clothes were stained in dirt, sweat, and blood. Motionless.

Jude ambled up toward Yosef, stretching his hand out, he wanted to be held. He yearned for security. Gripping along his bicep, Jude pulled himself toward Yosef, nuzzling his head against him. In a tender, fluid motion, Yosef draped his arm over Jude's shoulders and pulled him in close.

Jude looked through the audience and found the twins. For the first time, since he realized they were twins, he could tell neither Yeshua or Ta'oma apart. Both looked crestfallen, in mourning.

"*Yeshua!*" a blood-curdling scream ripped through the dense fog of grief.

Everyone jumped, some recoiled, protecting their children as they drew back.

"*Yeshua!*" came another screech.

Jude peered around some on-lookers to discover the weeping mother waving a taught finger at the twins. Her voice was frantic, raspy, and full of vitriol. The child's body in her arms bounced with each pronouncement, articulated and emphasized by the pointed finger.

With both sets of the twins' eyes on the woman, one stood behind the other with his arms wrapped around his brother. Jude then discovered which of the two was Yeshua.

With eyes firm and fixed on the woman, Yeshua raised a hand to dry his eyes. Ta'oma was talking in his ear as the woman screamed at them, his arms becoming tense and red. Yosef's arm unwrapped from Jude's shoulders, and with a quickened pace he stood between the twins and the woman.

Yosef raised his hands up, speaking in a calm, benevolent voice. Yeshua pulled Ta'oma's hands from his body, turning to face the woman with his hands behind his back. Yosef's attempts to calm the woman proved futile; the more he tried, the louder she raved. Breaking her glare from him and the boys only to reposition her dead child's body in her arms, the woman bordered on the brink of being unhinged.

Yosef's voice started to get louder; a temper started to peak out from his words.

Jude furrowed his brow. Not Yosef too.

As Yosef and the woman went back and forth, their attention going between themselves, the roof of the hut they stood in front of, and Yeshua, the crowd began to physically shift. Yeshua stepped between them, facing the woman. Startled by his sudden close proximity, both adults froze with their eyes locked on him.

Yeshua knelt before her, clasping his hands together, and he muttered something softly to her. With his arms outstretched, remorse in his eyes and tone, the woman passed her crumpled tissue of a son to Yeshua with shaky arms.

Taking the child and setting him in front of himself, Yeshua sobbed as he looked over the child. Jude raised a cautious eyebrow as he witnessed the exchange. This could not have been real; the Yeshua he had come to know would laugh at a moment like this. This was his Saturday morning cartoons, his snack after a long day at school, or the video games anyone in Jude's day would have enjoyed.

Stepping closer, Jude weaved between witnesses and their family members to get closer to the action. Bumping into one woman, Jude's 20th century manners took over.

"I'm so sorry," he blurted out. It was like he wasn't even there. The woman clasped a hand over her mouth and pointed forward with a trembling hand.

Turning around, Jude's jaw dropped to find the boy propping himself up on his elbows. One hand rubbed his eyes, he let out a small collection of gargled coughs.

The boy's mother hollered with vibrant enthusiasm. She fell forward in her excitement, arms thrust around the boy, squeezing him as if he might slip back into death. Placing her hands on the boy's cheeks, she turned his head to her and started speaking at a rapid-fire pace. The boy shook his head, pointing at the roof of the hut. With weak hand gestures, he pantomimed a story as his voice gave a raspy narration. It concluded with the boy turning his gaze to Yeshua and stating, "Mashiach."

Gasps came from several people.

A look of pride swelled over Yosef's face. His arms crossed in a smooth, triumphant gesture.

"*Mashiach...*" came another voice from the crowd.

"*Mashiach!*" shouted a third.

Whispers grew to murmurs, like waves crashing on the shore. Some started to rock as their hands clasped together in prayer. Several voices grew to hollers; arms raised up to the skies.

Jude's jaw slacked as his arms dangled by his sides. "H-how?" Jude stammered.

His jaw trembled as he fought to find the words.

"Ow!" Jude shouted. His knee came up to his chest as he clutched his ankle, suddenly burning like a hot needle was jabbed into his Achilles tendon.

It was slippery, and clumpy to the touch. Like a thin coat of cottage cheese. Bringing his hand up to his face, Jude found blood and a loose, greasy, yellow liquid tracing between the red streaks. Gazing at his ankle, he found two small puncture wounds behind his ankle bone, more blood and yellow grease trickling from them.

And then the familiar sound of a rattle.

6

"Yudah!" Yosef screamed.

Running at him, Yosef scooped up Jude. Another citizen lunged forward, lobbing off the snake's head.

"Rabbi!" Yosef hollered as he started to shove his way through the crowd. "Rabbi!"

The crowd shrieked and hollered, ducking out of the way. Jude looked down at his leg, bouncing up and down with each stride. It was swollen, throbbing. He started to sweat. Wiping the sweat from his upper lip, Jude noticed that his mouth had gone numb.

"Yosef," came a small, calming voice that pierced the crowd and stopped Yosef in his tracks. With a thundering authority, Yeshua's voice wrenched the heads of everyone toward him.

Jude's stomach churned as Yosef turned to face Yeshua. A path was still clear, leading from Yosef to Yeshua, whose hand was gesturing for Yosef to approach him. Jude's heart throbbed against his chest, stopping and starting like Morse code.

Stepping in front of Yeshua, Yosef's face remained statuesque and unflinching. He knelt, placing Jude before him on the ground. Retching on the ground beside him, Jude turned his head upward to catch Yeshua and Ta'oma standing over him. A scattering of voices swirled around him as he attempted to adjust his vision to the two silhouettes standing over him. Both of them waved their right arm in unison over Jude, moving together over him.

47

"Shit," coughed Jude, his breathing becoming labored and dry. Those weren't the twins, and that wasn't two people walking into view. He was seeing double.

"Venom..." Jude sputtered. His clothing now clinging to his clammy flesh, drenched in sweat. Things started to sound like echoes in a tunnel.

A rough bony hand gripped tightly around Jude's ankle. Retracting his knee in agony, the hand held strong. A pulsing, burning ache shot up his leg. Jude tried to scream, but a raspy whistle was all that escaped his throat.

As sudden as the pain rocketed through his body, a chill greeted Jude's leg. It was rain on a sunny August afternoon. Jude's throat retracted; his first breath in was as comforting as being in his mother's arms. Looking down, Yeshua was gripping Jude's leg with one hand, the other held up his weight. Light shone out of his eye sockets; sweat dripped from his brow as his mouth twitched in a whisper, too fast for Jude to make out any words. And then his eyes returned to normal, his irises fading in from pale white to a dark brown, teetering on black. And as they did, Yeshua collapsed in tears.

"Yudah," he cried. "Yudah."

Jude propped himself up on his elbows; saliva trickled down his face. Yeshua lay at his feet with his head in his hands. His breathing implied sobbing, and Jude pulled his feet toward himself. Perhaps he was upset at what had happened. Or, perhaps, he was setting up Jude to be his next victim.

With his heart racing, Jude crept his feet up and away from Yeshua. Some pebbles, stuck to his feet, fell as they moved through the air. The light tapping and rebounding of the pebbles may as well have been gunfire.

Yeshua pushed himself up so that he was resting on all fours. Tears, puffy red eyes, and drool painted Yeshua's face. His lip quivered as he gazed at Jude. "Yudah," he whimpered, climbing to his feet

"No," Jude fired back, raising his hand to stop him.

Yeshua dove for Jude, wrapping his arms around him, squealing for joy. Jude huffed and puffed as his squeezes and slaps continued. Then he realized, there were more than two arms holding, and lifting, him.

The murmurs of "*Mashiach*" started to ripple through the air.

Bringing him high up into the air, Jude found himself riding atop Yosef's shoulders. Shouting to the spectators, Yosef made some elaborate, official-sounding declaration. It was met by cheers, people giving joyous praise to the sky, to Yahweh. Yosef then turned, placing Jude on the ground as if he were an ancient artifact. In a calm and collected presentation, Yosef made an articulate statement. He ended with a look of great intrigue and concern.

Jude's eyes darted back and forth, between Yosef and the spectators.

"I-I'm sorry?" Jude asked. "I don't speak Hebrew. Not a lot, at least."

"*Aramaic*," came a calm voice behind him.

Jude jumped, twisting around with his hand against his chest. Yeshua stood before him, his hands behind his back, head bowed. Peering up at Jude, a smirk broke across his face.

"The name of the language they speak," said Yeshua. "Aramaic. It's kind of like Hebrew."

Jude shook his head. "Wait," he blurted out, stepping toward Yeshua. "You can—"

"How did it feel?" Yeshua interrupted.

"What?" Jude asked, stopping in his tracks.

"When the snake bit you," he continued. "What did you feel?"

Jude's breath became deep and heavy. His eyes searched the floor as he processed the question, all the while fighting off the urges for his video games and mother's embrace. His stomach knotted; tears dropped free from his cheeks almost unnoticed.

"Knives," was all Jude could articulate. "Knives made of flames."

"And?" Yeshua asked. "What of when you were healed."

Jude paused. He recalled the summers his parents took him to Cape Anne in Gloucester, Massachusetts. Even on the hottest days, going into the water was often like doing an ice plunge in February. The anticipation, the anxiety, the kind Jude loved. The worry of just how cold the water would be at first. And like a band aid, as soon as the jump into the water was made, the reality, the acceptance, was there. It was always like a million tiny sea crabs were stabbing you with ice shanks, but it was over as quickly as it started. And it always felt amazing after.

"The same," Jude replied. "Only with ice."

"Daggers?" Yeshua inquired.

Jude nodded.

Looking up at Yosef, Yeshua cleared his throat.

"Siqari'im," Yeshua said.

"What?" Jude asked. "What does that mean?"

Turning his head over his shoulder, Yeshua peered back at Jude.

"Daggers," he shrugged.

Yosef's eyes scurried back and forth, processing the information. And in a triumphant twirl, he faced the crowd with his fist in the air.

"Yudah ish krayot!" Yosef hollered into the crowd.

"Yudah ish krayot!" they proclaimed back. Cheers and shouts of praise broke out through the cries. People embraced one another. Smiles spread in excitement across people's faces. Their voices rang with anxious joy; some cried with tears moistening the lines of their faces, dampening the dust and dirt caked across their profiles.

Jude stared, dumbfounded. The name Yosef used for Jude, Yudah, had been the same one that the child in his room had used for him. The one who brought him here. Again, struck by how familiar it sounded, he wondered why the people rejoiced?

"*Your name*," came a now recognizable voice.

Jude spun around to catch Yeshua approaching him from behind.

"What about it?" Jude asked.

"You've been given your title," Yeshua replied. With his hands in the air, mimicking a billboard, he said "Jude of the Dagger."

With a wave of his hand, everyone stopped moving. As if he had slapped a giant pause button on an unseen remote. Not even a blink.

"Oh... Christ..." Jude murmured, too frightened to try to move.

"Perhaps you'd recognize the title by your modern translation," Yeshua continued.

Walking up to a resident of the village, in the process of leaping with his feet just barely having left the ground, Yeshua opened the flap to a handbag around the man's shoulder.

"What... what is it?" Jude demanded, whipping his head back and forth. Dumbfounded by the sight of people frozen in their tracks. "What's the title?"

Ignoring him, Yeshua had his head and one of his arms fully immersed in the man's bag. Muttering gibberish under his breath, Yeshua's tone flexed upwards. A sound of triumph, of positive results, purred out of the handbag. And Yeshua emerged with a wine skin.

Jude's pulse quickened. A feeling of sweet relief and calm came over him. "Can I..." he started. "I really need a drink."

Yeshua, stopping in front of Jude, looked down at the wine skin, pursing his lips, his brow in frustrated folds. His hand eventually extended, offering the skin to Jude.

"It hurts, because I know I shouldn't," said Yeshua as Jude snapped the wine skin from his hand. With his eyes full of lust, fixated on the cork, Jude's free hand struggled to emancipate from the skin. "But it's who you are," sighed Yeshua.

Jude, with feverish panting, ripped the cork from the skin and without hesitation introduced the contents to his mouth. The sharp bitterness of the wine made way for the calm placid relief Jude longed for. The voices dulled. The worries deadened. His fears numbed.

Pulling the skin from his lips, Jude wiped his mouth across the back of his free arm. "And who," he asked, "am I?"

Watching him take another swig from the wine skin, Yeshua smirked.

"Judas Iscariot."

7

"*Crucify him!*" came the chants.

"*Blasphemer!*"

"*Away with him!*"

The crowd moved like chaotic waves, in sporadic violent leaps. Fists stabbed through the air; cries for blood echoed across the stone and mortar surrounding them. Saliva, sweat, and anger hung thick in the atmosphere. Jude's eyes darted around the crowd looking for a familiar face. His head whipped from side to side. His brothers, his sisters, their parents, friends, none of them were present. Instead, angry strangers. People Jude felt he'd always seen in the crowds taunting his brother. Mobs demanding some type of justice, not knowing the full story.

As the waves of vitriol bobbed up and down, Jude noticed a platform in the distance. And on that platform stood a single, shaking figure.

It was Yeshua.

Beaten, bloody, and quivering from shock, Yeshua faced the crowd with a sleepy gaze. He swayed from side to side, jerking upright if he started to drift too far in one direction or the other. A puddle of blood formed around his feet. Rocks started flying at Yeshua from the crowd.

"*Ha-shatan!*" the voices bellowed.

Starting as small ripples, the voices evolved into a raging river of screams.

"Yeshua," Jude called, reaching his hand for the platform. He started pushing his way through the crowd. "Yeshua!"

The rocks skidded across the platform. Several connected with Yeshua. First, they hit his feet. Next, his legs, making a loud wet clapping sound. Yeshua flinched, losing his footing for a split-second. Forcing his way through, pushing people aside with frantic anxiety, Jude started to shout.

"Yeshua!" Jude hollered.

A deep purple light began to envelop Yeshua.

Jude came to an abrupt halt, squinting his eyes toward the now luminescent figure before him.

Rocks continued to rocket toward the stage.

Yeshua rose off of the platform, like a marionette pulled up by its strings. A low vibration, almost a hum, started to rattle inside Jude's head. A dark shadow fell over the crowd. Jude glanced up, expecting overcast. Instead, he was greeted by a dark orb sliding in conjunction over the sun.

Yeshua's head rose, his eyes like suns. Lightning flashed, startling Jude as it paired with an earth trembling thunder clap. The people around him shrieked. It was the continued screeching that frightened him.

Fire arose between the blood curdling hollers and flailing limbs. Looking to his right, Jude jumped as he watched the person next to him implode on himself. The man's flesh sagged like hot putty; blood oozed out from his eyes and holes that appeared and expanded. As his flesh melted away, the bones dropped like broken tree limbs, shattering into dust as they hit the ground. The piles of dust melted into puddles. After the flesh, blood, and body mass congealed into a puddle, it bubbled like boiled pudding, if for only a moment. It then shriveled and dissipated into a mist. Gone like breaths in the wind.

Jude whipped his head around. Some, like him, remained unaffected; reacting in horror at the chaos around them. Without warning, Jude lost his footing and dropped through a chasm that had opened beneath him. A soft, yellow light under him widened into a massive opening, revealing fire, screams, cries of agony, cries for God.

A dark silhouette with red eyes appeared, growing upwards as Jude shot down toward the massive, bipedal figure.

With horns.

Jude saw it open its mouth, as a piercing light fired out of the space. It felt like a sniper's scope guide and shot hitting him at once. The figure's hot, rancid breath struck Jude mere inches before the teeth slammed shut.

***

Jude shot up from his sleep, a cold sweat dripping down his face. Wiping his forehead with the back of his arm, cool droplets trickled down his limb, dropping with a soft *pat* sound as it hit the blanket tangled between his legs. His vision was blurry, head heavy, and the bitter taste of stale wine lingered in his mouth. His tongue felt sticky, gummy almost. Each breath felt heavy; an unnecessary amount of effort was expelled to take in each gasp of air. His eyes, irritated and unfocused, scoured the floor beside where he lay.

A wine skin, dripping wine in slow measure, drawings of figures and futuristic items from his past etched onto the floor. Jude struggled to remember the previous evening's events. Already, the guilt and shame were overwhelming.

"*Judas?*" came a worried call from the doorway.

Seeing Judith out of the corner of his eye, Jude combed through a patch of his scruffy beard with one hand. His eyes shot back and forth, his breath deep and focused.

"My Judas?" Judith called again. "How are you feeling?"

"I'm fine," he replied, continuing to scratch the same patch. His eyes continued to glance around the room.

Judith looked down, noticing the spot Jude's eyes kept moving to. "It's okay to be upset," Judith said, leaning down to pick up the wine skin.

Jude started to squirm, reaching out for the skin, stopping himself, and pulling away. Judith, still bent over, offered the skin to Jude.

"We are all affected by Father's loss," she whispered.

Tears dripped down Jude's face, his hands slammed against the ground as his face squeezed shut into a sour grimace. A hand clasped with gentle pressure around Jude's chin, directing it upwards. His eyes met with Judith's; the deep, dark brown of her irises were scarred with heavy streaks of red lightning. Jude could barely make out the wet remainder of tears that sparkled down her cheeks.

"He…" she started, her voice shaky. "He will be among the first to rise up and join us when God's Kingdom arrives." She touched the wine skin to Jude's lips. "We need to be strong for him," she whispered, raising the skin up.

The wine poured like honey down Jude's throat. With the first taste of wine, Jude always saw and heard the moment in cartoons when Popeye would eat spinach to take on a challenge. He felt it. His motivation, his energy, his ability to think, all came front and center once the first few swallows of wine hit the back of his throat.

"My Judas," Judith whispered, kissing his forehead. "Be strong. Your time has almost come."

Jude pulled the skin from his lips, heavy panting, licking his lips. "Has he…" he started, catching his breath. "Has he returned yet?"

"No," Judith replied. "But…"

A young man with a patchy beard burst into the room from behind Judith. He gripped her shoulders and bounced up and down with excitement. His face red and puffy.

"Simon!" cried Judith, regaining her balance.

"He's here," Simon exclaimed before sniffing back up mucus and forcing a smile on his face. He gestured for them to go outside, sprinting back out of the hut.

Judith rose up, offering her hand to Jude. He sucked at the end of the wine skin, grasping her hand as the last of the beverage rattled out of the opening. As he rose, the blanket dropped away exposing his bare body to Judith. With a soft cry, she turned her head, covering her eyes. Jude frantically grabbed at the cloth, waving one hand in front of his genitals. With a gentle laugh she walked out of the room. A damp, but clean piece of clothing was tossed through the doorway.

Jude threw the tunic on. Mary must have had it out on the line after washing it in the rain. Or perhaps it was the tunic worn by Joseph as he had gone to the bath house, anticipating his inevitable death.

Jude emerged from the family's hut, the sun punching down on him with blistering heat. His eyes burned even from the reflection of the sun from the sand. He started to sweat again. Looking up, the neighbors were all looking in the same direction. A few, noticing Jude, squinted at him in disappointment and turned back to their chores or went inside their homes. Jude followed the gaze of the others. There was his family, crying in excitement as a blurry figure marched toward them with hands in the air.

Jude heard someone say, "...*even his family thinks he's crazy. I've heard them say it.*" Peering around the corner, he spotted two young boys watching the greeting. Giggling and elbowing one another, they taunted the family.

"He keeps talking about a new kingdom," said one.

"My father says he can go back to his stupid kingdom," the other responded. "We don't need him and their kind here."

Jude stood out in front of them.

"Matthew and Luke," came Jude's stern announcement. They gasped, looking up at him. "Are you sure that's wise?" he asked.

The boys stuttered, struggling to find a response.

"You know the stories of what my brother has done to children who questioned him," he continued.

The boys glanced at each other.

"Which one of you wants to confirm them?"

Both boys gasped, pivoted, and ran out of sight.

Jude belched, coughing out a wad of red phlegm. Looking up at the sky, Jude sighed. "Elisha got bears, but none for me?" he chuckled and marched toward his family.

Mary's cries could be heard well before Jude was close to them. He could see Mary rocking back and forth as she embraced the figure. Simon stood beside her, jumping up and down excitedly with his arms around both of them.

Judith and Rachel stood by, their hands clasped together, hugging as they watched the greeting.

"Where's Thomas?" asked Jude, rubbing his eyes as he scanned the landscape.

"Gone to see Rabbi John," replied Rachel. "He should be home by nightfall."

"James is in prayer," said Judith, gesturing with her head toward the modest home of the community's rabbi.

Jude scowled at the house.

"Judas," Judith cooed, poking his arm with her elbow. "Be happy. He's returned."

"I am," Jude growled.

Tears shimmered on Simon's face as he spoke, rapid fire, about milestones he'd reached. Studying with Rabbi John. Rejecting lustful thoughts. Ensuring he paid his taxes for fishing in Galilee. Jesus beamed with pride over his younger brother. His hair having grown significantly longer, his beard a tangled drape over his throat. The clothing he wore was splotched with dirt, sand, and sweat. Jesus' skin looked wrinkled and rough. Jude wished for a drink while studying him.

"Simon," Jesus declared. He pressed his forehead against Simon's. "You are my rock. You are the rock for all this!" He waved his hand over the town. Simon's face reddened as his smile appeared to grow bigger than his face.

"My brother," Jude called.

Jesus looked up and smiled as his eyes met with Jude. Rubbing Simon's back, his arms extended out to Jude.

"Judas," he laughed, taking large steps toward him. "My beloved..."

As their bodies crashed together, Jude felt the comfort, the security, of Jesus' embrace. Even with the rank odors emanating from him, the fact that it was Jesus holding him was comfort enough.

Jude remembered the hugs he had been forced to give relatives. They always joked that the hug wasn't good enough, forcing a full-on bear hug. Pins and needles crept up Jude's back during those imprisoning moments. His right ring finger would twitch, sometimes his whole hand, during involuntary intervals. Though he wouldn't feel it, his legs would be tired, as if he'd been sprinting. Maybe his body reacted that way because it was preparing to run while unable to escape. But not with Jesus. Jesus' hugs were unique. They felt authentic. Even when Jude felt like he didn't want a hug, or wasn't sure what he needed or wanted, Jesus' hugs always felt apt.

"I'm so proud of you," Jesus hummed in Jude's ear.

Jude pulled Jesus in closer, as tears suddenly crept down into his beard.

"I've missed you," Jude whispered.

"And I you," Jesus replied, with a soft kiss on Jude's cheek.

As Jesus pulled away, Jude grabbed his arm. Looking at Jude, Jesus' eyebrows were furrowed in concern, his mouth agape.

"It's Joseph," Jude whimpered. His shoulders shook as he choked back the sobs that sat in his throat.

Jesus' hand came up and rested on Judas' arm. "I knew," Jesus said.

59

"You always know," Jude wept. "Yet you never warn us. You never..."

"I provide you with exactly what you need," Jesus said, squeezing Jude's arm. His voice was stern and unshaken.

Arms wrapped over both men's shoulders as Mary's face came in between them, her face torn between expressing joy and despair. "My boys," her voice a gentle nudge, "My Lords, please come and sit. My prodigal son has returned."

The men embraced, Jude snorting up the drizzle that ebbed and weaved through his thick, dark facial hair. Pulling apart, arm-in-arm, they walked together. Jude wiped his face against his arm, Jesus chuckled.

"Brother," called Rachel, jogging up behind them with Judith.

Jesus looked over his shoulder at the girls. He raised his eyebrows and smirked at them.

"Did you meet with our father?" she asked.

Jesus' face turned morose and he started to look away.

"Jesus," Judith announced.

They all stopped.

Jesus, spinning on his heel, quickened his pace toward Judith.

"Child," he spoke with a dark, authoritative tone.

Stopping mere inches from Judith, his hands came up and clasped around Judith's chin. "We shall not fear the use of Father's name," he said, kissing her on the lips. "Instead we must fear those who do not understand us. Those who do not realize how history will look upon them."

Jude tried to swallow the mass that suddenly formed in his throat. His hand began to quake.

"J-Jesus..." Jude stammered.

Jesus turned back, his eyes widening with fear. Judith gasped. Jude fell to his knees as his whole body quaked. Jesus released Judith's face and both raced to catch Jude. Simon caught Jude by the back of his garb,

60

dropping to catch his chest before he landed in the dirt. Jude grunted as he was stopped by Simon, dropping to his side without warning.

"Wine!" Jesus hollered at Rachel, who was already sprinting away, looking for help.

They propped Jude up on his side, drool puddling through his beard. His eyes rolled back in his head; his body shook as if an electric current was flowing through him.

"*Jesus!*" they heard a call.

"Thomas," Jesus cried. "Wine!"

There was a hustle, movement, jostling. Jude suddenly found himself sitting up with a familiar taste. A comforting burn that felt like a warm blanket on the forgotten cold winter nights from back home.

Jude grasped the wine skin pressed to his lips, interlocking his fingers with the hand that held up the skin. His other hand found the ground, and he fought to find his balance as he imbibed like a dehydrated animal. His vision, evolving from a soft blurring of his surroundings to crystal clear, found a concerned Jesus and a smiling Thomas.

"You're a wonder," Thomas chuckled. "Look at what you do! Rabbi John was right. No wonder James hates you."

"Thomas," Jesus said. "That isn't something we should celebrate. If hate is in his heart, then he is no better than a murderer."

"*The prodigal son returns,*" came a boisterous voice from behind them. All of them looked toward where the voice came from.

"James," growled Simon.

James stood by the path in a dark tunic with matching headdress. His beard, spotted with flakes of gray, was long and wavy draping across the upper half of his chest. As he stepped forward, his clothing rippled like little ringlets of black water. Dust kicked up in miniature brown tornadoes.

"James?" called Simon. "James, look who's come back!"

"Our own Caesar Augustus," sneered James. "What did your Father tell you this time, blasphemer?"

61

"Know your place," cried Thomas, stepping in between the two men.

"Peasant," snickered James. His lip curled up to reveal dark red, tender gums with pale yellow teeth. Looking up at Jesus, his smile turned to a frown. "What did your Father show you, son of David?" asked a facetious James.

Leaning in toward James, a smile across his face, Jesus sighed. "James," he huffed out, hanging his head, "the treasures that were promised to me by *shatan* could not be imagined by any mortal alive."

Jude, suckling the few remaining drops from the wine skin, lowered his arms straining focus on Jesus.

"*Shatan* offered me wealth," Jesus carried on, pulling Thomas out from between them. "Power. Authority. I was offered a chance to be God."

James' eyes bulged, his brow forced inward; the corners of his mouth bolted into position.

"Do you know why Thomas returned so joyful?" Jesus asked James, his tone soft and warm.

"Because you fill his head with lies," James grunted out.

"James," Jesus replied. "All those times you second guessed my prophecies, the time you spent calling me crazy to our teachers, our neighbors, for what?"

Scoffing at the accusation, James crossed his arms and shook his head, looking down.

"Each prediction I have made," continued Jesus, "has come true. You have seen me heal the sick, exorcise demons…"

"Who would not have been there," James erupted, "had you not put them into your sheep followers."

"And why would I cause undue suffering?" asked Jesus. "Why harm others to build myself up? Especially when—"

"Don't you say it," James hollered, a thick finger thrust into Jesus' face. "Save your blasphemy for when you reach the gates of Gehenna."

"Should I be judged so harshly because of my desire to help those afflicted?" Jesus asked.

"None may heal, none may forgive, but El," hissed James.

"And yet," smiled Jesus, "here I stand." He gestured at Jude. "And I have healed."

"Jesus," spoke Thomas, shaking his head. "What you asked me to check on?"

Without breaking his eye contact with James, Jesus replied. His eyes welled with tears. "It's…" he swallowed. "It's happened, hasn't it?"

"Yes," came Thomas' reply.

Jesus raised his head upward as he fought back tears. Taking a deep inhale through his nose, he wiped away the droplets as they left his eyes.

"What?" demanded James. "What is it?"

"My time has come," Jesus forced out. Turning to Jude, he said, "It's time we had a conversation."

"Wait," James insisted. "What do you mean? What did you have my brother do? What was he checking on? Be concise now, agitator, or I'll have the authorities stone you in public."

"No, you won't," Jesus replied. "And I know you will one day regret those words, so I forgive you."

Sneering at Jesus, James turned his back to his brothers and started to walk away.

"James," Jesus called after him. "John is dead."

James stopped, turning back toward Jesus. He looked at Thomas, who nodded to confirm.

"Herod," Jesus stated. "Beheaded."

James displayed no change in attitude or mental state. With no noticeable difference in affect, he turned and continued on his way. "Tell Mother I say goodbye," he announced.

8

"John is dead," Jesus announced over the murmurs around the fire. Sloshing of beverages, soft tearing of bread between the jaws of tired, hungry laborers. And then nothing but the crackling of the fire. All turned and faced Jesus. "Beheaded," he continued. "Herod ordered it himself."

"*So, we are finished?*" came a voice across the circle.

Jude leaned up against Simon, who was seated next to Jesus. "Peter..." Jude grumbled, fumbling with his chalice.

With a smirk, Simon looked down at Jude. "My Lord," he replied.

"You smug ass," Jude chuckled. "Brother calls you his rock, and suddenly it's your name?"

"I think it's well deserved," Simon smiled, knocking back the last of his wine.

"No," announced Jesus. "Anything *but* finished."

"Then what are we to do?" hollered one man, standing up, drinking from his cup.

"Bartholomew," Jesus pleaded. "it's not as you fear."

"Isn't it?" Bartholomew exclaimed. "Our Messiah is dead. Please tell me where the Ketuvim says our Messiah will be beheaded?"

"Oh, look at me," Jude said in a mocking tone. "I'm Peter, the rock of our faith!"

"Now you're just being cruel," said Simon, gazing into his cup.

"I'm sorry," said Jude, tapping the bottom of his glass as he held it, upended, over his mouth.

Simon sighed. "You're not."

"You know I am," snapped Jude, repulsed at the notion.

"He wasn't it," said Jesus. His hands raised as if anticipating Bartholomew would swing at him.

"*Who then?*" came another voice. A taller, more well-groomed man stood beside Bartholomew. "Who is our Messiah, if it were not Rabbi John?"

"Levi," Jesus called. "I'm happy to…"

"There is no one," Levi shouted. Others groaned and clapped in response.

"Quiet yourself," Jesus commanded. "John was an example for the rest of us."

"You quiet yourself, swine," snapped Levi.

"Not when you've had enough wine to drown a mule," groaned Simon.

"You don't honestly know how much that would take," said Jude, gazing up at Jesus and Levi.

"Oh, like that's even the point, Judas," Simon chuckled. He reached behind Jesus and grasped one of several wine skins, shaking his head in amusement.

Jude's arm stretched in front of Simon, shaking his glass in his face.

"Of course, my dear," Simon cooed.

"How dare you," Jesus rose to his feet. "No one has held more devoutly to the words of our Lord than I."

"You are a charlatan," Levi protested.

"*Watch your tone,*" came a woman's voice. Judith rose, her hand pointing at Levi. "For he is Jesus, son of Joseph, descendant of our great King David."

"Here comes the real patriarch of the home, to the rescue," called Levi.

The others snickered.

Simon filled Jude's glass, a smirk on his face. "You know how I love you?" asked Simon. Jude grunted, a single eyebrow raised. "I don't listen to your enemies who besmirch your good name," Simon smiled, elbowing Jude. Jude smirked, eyes still fixed on Jesus. He slurped from the top of the glass. Simon bit his lip. "But I worry about you," he confessed.

"It is not until we can shed these titles," Jesus proclaimed. "'Man'... 'woman'... these are titles we have given ourselves. These are titles Adam, not God, bestowed on us. If we want to welcome our Father's kingdom—"

"You fool," shot back Levi. "We will be sent to Gehenna before God's kingdom comes."

"He who uses slurs like 'fool' will be the first cast into the flame," Judith snapped.

"Why?" Jude asked Simon, swallowing a mouthful of wine.

"Because it's not until you're this drunk that I feel I can tell you these things," said Simon. Placing the wineskin back behind Jesus, he sighed.

"You can tell me anything, anytime," Jude slurred.

"Of course," Simon rolled his eyes. "And my name's Rocky."

"Are you just going to allow her to speak that way?" demanded Bartholomew.

"She may speak as any other member of our community," Jesus' voice became stern. "She has worked and contributed just as hard, if not harder, than any other apostle seated here."

"What?" hollered Levi. More men started to stand up, glaring at Jesus. "Do you question the effort of the rest of us? Of us men?"

Several women stood, gathering behind Jesus. Some with clenched fists and looks of defiance etched into their faces.

"You know that's not what I said," Jesus said. "And we're not discussing what needs to be addressed."

"I didn't know that a plan was needed when the ship sinks," hollered Levi. "Like rats, we'll all just either learn to swim or sink."

"Are you even listening to me?" Simon asked, nudging Jude. Jude waved at him, his head rotating from side to side as he realized what was happening.

"Simon," Jude whispered.

Simon looked around, his eyes widening as the gravity struck him. Both stood up, Jude edging closer to Jesus to extinguish any concern of which side he was on.

"Do not vilify our movement," Jesus warned. "And watch your voice. You forget that we are guilty by association with Rabbi John."

"I don't have to," blurted out Levi. "When half the membership are children of the village mason and the eldest works for the Pharisees."

"James has had noth—" Judith started to say.

"Shut your mouth, whore!" Levi shouted.

Jude's knees buckled, overcome with emotion. Simon caught him, helping him to the ground. "Stop shouting," Jude pleaded through sobs. His body shook.

Jesus, watching Jude, gripped his fist in his hand. "Do not address my family so disrespectfully," Jesus warned.

"Or what?" shouted Levi.

Jude jerked his knees up into his chest. Simon shushed him, stroking his hair.

"You are causing unnecessary suffering," Jesus said. "And it's at my family's expense. I have been reasonable and patient with you…"

Levi grabbed a log from the fire, pegging it at Jesus. The women shrieked. Simon threw himself over Jude. Jesus, without flinching, held his hand up as the log disappeared into a black vapor. As if a magic trick had occurred, all stood speechless, staring at Jesus.

The soothing crackle of the fire and familiar chirps of nighttime insects were all that filled the raucous silence. Even Jude's labored breathing had slowed as he attempted to listen.

"Who…" choked out Bartholomew. "Who are you?"

Jude started to rise to his feet. Judith stepped in front of Jesus, vindication in her eyes.

"He was sent by He who is called 'I am,'" Judith growled.

There were audible gasps, murmurs

"Demon," snapped Levi. "Words spoken by the *shatan*!"

"Enough," Jesus' words seemed to shake the earth. His right hand raised up in front of him, his eyes began to glow.

Levi lifted off the ground.

Simon smiled.

Jude turned to Jesus, reaching for his arm. "Brother," he cried.

Jesus' hand spread out, making Levi thrust his limbs out in a spread-eagle position. "I have allowed you to speak your piece," Jesus said. "Yet you attack my family. You disparage my bloodline." Levi struggled, his face contorting into depictions of terror and agony. "My family," Jesus said, exasperated. "You take issue with me, so address me."

Levi's face stretched out, as far as his muscles would allow him. A stuttered breathless scream sputtered out of his mouth. Two small dark stains formed on his tunic, around the tops of his shoulders. As Levi's screams became more abrasive, the stains grew in size.

"I am a shepherd to my fellow Jews," declared Jesus. "But to those who do not believe..." He waved his hand and Levi's tunic ripped off of his body and collapsed to the ground. His emaciated torso was covered in a thin layer of blood. Starting just under his collar bones, a uniform incision formed, crossing over his sternum, and meeting at a point above his groin. It formed a fish. "I am a fisher of men," Jesus said.

"Fuck," Jude murmured.

Jesus raised his other hand, gesturing with his palm face up. Levi hollered, his stomach tensing and flexing. Jesus wiggled the tips of his fingers, and Levi squealed as an audible tearing noise was heard. Blood started to cascade down Levi's groin.

"Did John not warn you, tax collector?" Jesus' eyes seemed to glow brighter. "No man can serve both God and money."

68

The almond shape of flesh between the incision started to separate, like a gory Velcro strap on a child's shoe.

"Jesus!" cried Jude.

Levi's cries turned into wails and weeping.

"And they will see the son of man coming in clouds with great power and glory," Jesus announced.

Blood fell from Levi's body in cascades of crimson sheets. The tearing of flesh made a sound that, with a hard enough tug, made Levi squirm and gag. Several of those seated around the fire, turned and wretched with violence.

A trembling hand placed itself on Jesus' shoulder. "Please…" Jude whispered. "*Mashiach…*"

Jesus' eyes appeared to snap into focus. Shaking his head, he looked up at Levi; his head bowed, breathing quick and labored. He had grown pale and appeared to be rotting. Internal bleeding had created dark pockets along his skin.

Jesus closed his eyes, one of his fingers danced and swirled in a soft pattern. Levi's skin began to roll back down over his abdomen, an almost instant fusion of the flap and his stomach. The color returned to his skin, and the pockets of brown and purple across Levi's body faded.

Lowering his arms, Jesus watched as Levi was guided to the ground with a soft shuffle of the sand as he attempted to gain his footing. He stumbled to the ground, his robe hanging from his waist, a reddish-pink scar took up the entire front of Levi's bony frame. Sweat drizzled down several paths along Levi's torso; his eyes flickered as he struggled to hold himself up. Several of the others jumped to catch him. Some of the voices clamored with speculation, a fog of anxiety spread through the site.

"What did you say to him?" asked a nervous voice behind Jude. He turned to find a wide-eyed Simon staring up at him. Jude swallowed back the lump that had appeared in his throat. He couldn't tell if it was because of how Simon looked at him, or because he was fighting back vomiting.

"Ma-" Jude swallowed, wiping at his mouth with the back of his hand. "Mashiach. Messiah."

Simon grinned and a nervous chuckle escaped his mouth. "You… you really think…" Simon said through scoffs.

"No!" Jude's voice reverberated off the hills around them. All others around the fire grew silent and turned their attention toward Jude and Simon. Jude, staggering to maintain his balance as he pushed himself away from Simon, turned his head toward Jesus. "I know who you are," he slurred.

Jesus smirked.

"And who do you say that I am?" Jesus asked, looking at Jude through the tops of his eyes.

Jude laughed. "You're the Messiah," he said.

His statement, met with silence, hung over the group.

"Judas," Simon called from behind him. "How do you know?"

"He's the Son of God," Judas blurted out.

"Enough!" yelled Bartholomew from across the fire.

"The Son of Man!" Jude continued. "The High Priest!"

"Stop!" cried Simon.

"The Ruler of the Coming Kingdom," Jude growled, taking a large swig from a newly opened wine skin.

"Fool!" bellowed Bartholomew. "Why do you think Rabbi John is gone?"

"He was careless," Jude said. "Acting during the day, at a public and holy site."

"Bite your tongue, blasphemer," grunted Levi, hunched over himself, gripping his stomach.

"Or what?" Jude taunted. "You dare challenge the beloved son of Joseph, brother of Jesus? Jesus the Messiah? The worker of true wonders?"

"Pride will only ensure your downfall, sinner," called out Levi.

"Pride?" demanded Jude. "You know not of which you speak."

Those around the fire chuckled in small groups.

"Are we Greek now?" asked Bartholomew. "You sound like those intellectuals who act like their books know more than those who experience the suffering they say we deserve."

"I would call you a child," Jude said. "but that would be a slight to the child."

"Indeed," Jesus chimed in, standing between Jude and their antagonists. "In order to enter the Kingdom, one must act as humble as children."

"W-what?" Bartholomew stammered.

"Children must prostrate themselves before others," Jesus continued, stepping toward Bartholomew. "They humble themselves, looking up to others, watching. They are curious, they bear no prejudices, and they seek to learn from those in their family."

Levi stood up and stepped forward, his fists clenched like knots on a ship's mast. Jesus held up his hand, and Levi complied.

"Moreover," Jesus continued, "the father, the head of the home, protects the women and children of his tribe. With the coming of God's Kingdom, I am sent by he who is called 'I AM.'"

"*Where is James?*" called someone behind Levi and Bartholomew.

The soft crisscrossing of murmurs dissipated as promptly as it had started.

"I am not my brother's keeper," Jesus snapped. "He has chosen greed over God."

"*You disparage the name of James the Just?*" called another voice shrouded in darkness.

Jude thrust himself in front of Jesus. "You cannot disparage what is true," Jude belched. "Just as you mistake my confidence for pride, you confuse fact with myth."

Turning to face Jesus, Jude gripped him by the collar. "Behold, I have finally seen it with my own eyes," he proclaimed. "The Son of Man, who came down in the clouds from Heaven with power…"

"He speaks the words of the prophets," Judith chimed in. "Daniel saw the coming of Jesus."

"No!" called Jude. "I did."

"You are no Maccabeus," Levi said, a smile spreading across his face.

"Nor do I profess to be," Jude laughed. "I have just seen what others have not."

"What is this you claim?" Jesus asked. "Is this prophecy?"

Jude, making eye contact with Jesus, felt his lip tremble. "My brother," his voice quivered. "What they will do to you—"

"I know," hushed Jesus.

"What does he mean?" Simon demanded. "Who are 'they?' What is it they're going to do?"

"Jesus," demanded Levi. "What does he mean?"

"I don't think…" Jesus started.

"He will die for the sins of man," Jude wept.

"Judas?" called Judith.

"No man can…" Levi said.

"Are you a Pharisee now?" Jude hollered at Levi. "You sound like the fanatics that pray in the streets, but go home to their young boys like the Gentile hypocrites."

"Judas!" Simon shouted.

"Get behind me Satan!" Jude blurted back, his finger stuck prominently in Simon's face. "I know who you are, and I know what you'll do."

Simon's face contorted into horrified expressions of disgust. "What is the meaning of this?" Simon demanded.

"Brother," Jude said in a near whisper. "I love you, and your passion. But when you are tested, you will deny your own blood."

Simon swallowed, shaking his head, eyes bulging out of their sockets at Jude. "Never," Simon announced.

"Three times," Jesus interrupted.

All heads turned and locked on Jesus.

Simon, exasperated, scoffed at Jude. "You doubt my allegiance?" demanded Simon. "Your own brother? Your rock...?"

"I do not doubt any such thing," said Jesus. "And I understand why you will do it."

"Brother—" pleaded Simon.

Jesus' hand rose up to stop him. "It is important that you do," Jesus reassured him. "If you don't, they will kill you. And then who would carry on our work when I'm gone?"

"Jesus..." Simon's eyes filled with tears. "You don't mean... I won't let—"

"They will," Jesus placed a hand on his shoulder. "And it's important you let it happen."

Simon mouthed a painful "no" as he pulled on Jesus' clothes.

"The suffering servant..." Judith said softly behind them.

Jesus, holding Simon under one arm, reached behind him and pulled Judith closer. The others, seated around the fire, looked to one another for answers. Low murmurs wove through the crackles of the fire and swishing of glasses and pitchers of wine.

"What is this?" demanded Bartholomew. "We have someone clearly influenced by Beelzebub who—"

"Don't you start," Jude snapped at Bartholomew. "I know what the future holds, and that future is one centered on our brother, Jesus." He took another swig from his glass, wiping his mouth on the back of his arm.

"Says the drunk," Levi sneered at him.

"You hated John because he never touched wine," Jude said. "You said he likely fornicated like a woman. Did you know he dressed as Elijah did?"

Jude instinctively threw a middle finger up at Levi. Confused looks and raised eyebrows were all he got in return, before putting his hand down. It was something he couldn't shake from before coming back in time. Without the offended outcome, it never had as satisfying an effect for him.

A hand gently found itself resting on Jude's shoulder. Turning around in a slow, purposeful motion, Jude found Jesus standing behind him. An entertained smirk sat on his face. "My brother holds far more talents than I think he lets on," Jesus said to the men opposing him. "It is either foresight, or mind reading. Either are fabulous abilities." Jesus chuckled, a gesture mirrored by a few others standing around him.

"I must do something terrible," Jude whimpered through gushing eyes. "Jesus…"

"Judas has been gifted with a vision few others see," Jesus continued, looking down into Jude's eyes. "And he knows the terrible cost."

The murmurs grew into frantic concern.

"*Will you be persecuted?*" A voice in the darkness rang out.

"We all will," said Judith, wiping a tear from her cheek.

Jesus looked to Jude, whose face was damp with sweat.

"I must do something terrible…" Jude mouthed at Jesus.

Jesus glanced down at the ground, shaking his head. When he looked back up at Jude, a frustrated, yet determined, look adorned his face.

"Brothers and sisters," Jesus called.

"*What?*" Someone cried out. Small batches of laughter broke through the group.

"Brothers and sisters?" Bartholomew emerged from the nay-sayers. "Perhaps your 'brothers and sisters' should take you home. Someone like you—"

Jude swung and connected with the side of Bartholomew's head. A loud crack and both men dropped, Jude clutching his wrist. Others gathered over them, lifting them up, analyzing their respective wounds.

Simon lifted Jude, Judith helping to support him up. His hand, barely more than a silhouette in the dark, appeared disfigured and wretched.

Jesus approached the men with stern, intentional steps. Raising his hands, one over each man, the sound of little pops and snaps permeated the air around them. Jude recalled the familiar sound like the bubble wrap his mother used to give to him when her shipments arrived. Pain shot up his arm like a hot knife dragged along his skin. Each pop produced a strike of lightning up his limb.

After a moment, the popping reduced, the pain almost unnoticeable. Jude's arm started to feel like a waking limb. He peered up at Jesus in time to see the bright lights from his eyes fade, his hands lowering with a swirling of lights like illuminated puffs of smoke.

Bartholomew rubbed at his jaw, incredulous to the circumstances. He looked back and forth between Jesus and his hands, his breath coming out in short exasperated gasps. Jesus looked at Bartholomew through his nose, his arm reaching back over Jude's shoulder. Jude rubbed his hand, flexing it and turning it over and back to analyze it.

"You should not doubt this man," Jesus said, squeezing Jude closer. "He was granted divine knowledge from a young age. This is why my family welcomed him into our home. Were his name not a sign from the Almighty, then his knowledge truly is."

Soft murmurs weaved through the group. Jude glanced behind him to make eye contact with Judith, her gaze authoritative and her posture demanding of respect. His heart rate quickened; his face flushed. Tears dropped down Judith's cheeks, their paths reflected by the fire. Jude had the sudden urge to embrace her. His body weight starting to shift toward Judith, Jesus pulled and squeezed Jude back in toward himself. Pulling his head closer to Jude's face, Jesus whispered, "Come away with me and I will tell you the mysteries of the kingdom."

Nodding, Jude stopped pressing toward Judith and stood upright.

"Our leadership, our *Messiah*," Jesus announced. "He is gone. We remain. Rabbi John has gone to await the induction of the New Jerusalem. He and those who have gone to rest will be the first to rise up to the heavens to greet the Son of Man when he comes. Either follow me, or join the hypocrite Pharisees like my brother and be content with your choice to be exiled once again from our promised home."

Turning his back to the others, Jesus guided Jude away from the fire. All remained silent, but the dimming fire which filled the vexatious silence that followed with comforting pops and snaps. Jude shook as he walked forward. He began to feel a knot in his chest tighten, his muscles ached. His teeth felt as if they might crack from clenching, and grinding, them with feverish fervor. He felt Jesus' hand come off his shoulder, rubbing gently between Jude's shoulder blades.

"I know why you are grieved," Jesus said.

Jude gasped as tears started to erupt from his eyes.

"You will no doubt suffer, as I will," Jesus reassured him, "but yours will be brief."

9

Wiping his red, irritated eyes across his arm, Jude took a deep swig from his half-empty wine skin.

"Stop," Jesus pleaded.

Looking down at the ground, Jude's arm that held the wine skin went limp. He rubbed his face in his free hand.

"You know what you're asking me to do," Jude sobbed. "You can't know what—"

"And you know my fate as well," Jesus quipped. Raising his hand, a faint trail of light followed his movements.

A small hole appeared out of nowhere. Like a fabric tearing, the hole grew into a wide-opened portal. Jude's breath caught in his throat. Aside from a gentle hum, no sound came from the portal. Instead, Jude watched a much younger version of himself, sitting and playing video games.

"My God…" Jude muttered. "My God, my God, my God…"

Jude watched his younger self jump, shake his head, and return to gameplay. One of his parents must have slammed their hands on the table, broken a dish, or slammed a door. Another similar-seeming portal emerged behind himself. Out walked the young boy who had put him in this mess.

If it weren't for him… Jude thought. He lunged toward the portal, which snapped shut, disappearing without a trace. "No!" Jude shouted.

Turning to Jesus, Jude ran at him, grabbing him by the collar.

"What are you?" Jude demanded. "Why did this happen? Why am I to be turned into this monster?"

Jesus' eyes widened in horror; his mouth slacked open.

"Monster?" Jesus asked. "Whatever do you mean?"

"My name," Jude said. "People use my name to call others traitor, or betrayer. All the people I grew up around, who said they followed your word, belittled me for being a Jew. They called me 'Christ killer.' They called me Judas. They—"

"But now you know," Jesus interrupted. "It is you."

"You're my brother," Jude pleaded. "I can't..." he shook his head. His shoulders shook as he tried to hold back tears.

"You must," Jesus reassured him. He rubbed Jude's arm and sighed. "I can heal your physical ailments," Jesus said. "I cannot, however, control your emotions."

"What is that?!" Jude hollered, shoving Jesus back. "From childhood I watched you maim, kill, torture, and then bring someone back from the dead. And you pushed them off the roof of the hut!"

"I did no such thing," Jesus hollered.

The environment turned ominous and rich with anxiety. Jude's breath became heavy and labored; he felt as if a boulder sat on his chest. Jesus' hand, with a trailing aura of light, waved at the air next to them, and a new portal opened. Peering into the opening, Jude saw children playing. Among them were a young Jesus, Thomas, and James. Jesus was playing in a hole with water. Something started splashing and Jesus, for a moment, appeared panicked. Looking around as he struggled with whatever was in the pit.

Jude looked over at Jesus, who shrugged.

"I like animals," Jesus said.

Jude looked around the scene. Aside from his three brothers, there were a few other children running around.

"Where is he?" Jude asked. "No one's on the roof."

Jesus brought a finger up to his lip. Pointing the same finger at the portal, Jesus whispered, "Watch."

Jude turned his gaze back to the portal. A cat ran out of the hole a young Jesus was elbow deep in. He looked fearful as he glanced around, trying to see if anyone noticed. James and Thomas appeared to be playing a tag game with some other children. With a static flash, one of the children disappeared. Thomas and James darted their heads around, looking to locate their lost companion. Another bright light flashed from overhead, and the boy's body came slamming down to the earth.

"You did do it," Jude said.

"No," Jesus responded.

Holding out his hand, turning it in a counter-clockwise motion, the scene reversed until it restarted with the three boys playing. Swinging his hand to the right, the sight was reframed to view the village to the left of the scene where the boys played. Another portal opened, and out of it came a man, short in stature, with long, dark, braided hair. He sported harem pants, worn-out, beaten sandals; he was bare-chested, with a beard that rested just above his sternum

"Behold," said Jesus. "My father."

The man they watched raised a hand, as Jesus had a moment before. A flash in the foreground snapped in and out of existence, and the young boy fell from the sky. The portal closed, flashing shut like an old television set.

Turning to Jesus, Jude swallowed a lump in his throat. "What is this?" he asked in earnest.

"The others are drawing near," Jesus warned. "Here…"

Raising his hand again, another portal opened, revealing a brick room with a dangling light.

Jude paused. "You want me to walk through there?" he demanded.

"Trust me," Jesus urged him. "We don't have time to argue, and we must go now."

Jesus pushed Jude from behind. Jude panicked, digging his heels into the ground. "No!" he shouted. Gripping at Jesus' hair, scratching at his face, doing anything to prevent him from being forced through another portal. Sweat broke out over his brow, his heart rate quickened, his breath strained and shallow. Approaching the edge of the portal, Jude started to flail his arms, stomping his feet against the ground in an attempt to project them backward.

"My apologies, brother," Jesus grunted. And he shoved Jude through the portal.

It was only for a brief moment, but it was like the sensation Jude imagined falling into a black hole provided. All he had to inform his perspective was the campy Disney movie he watched numerous times as a child. Jude recalled all the memories from when he first was forced through a portal. He thought about the day he was removed from the comfort of his home, when he lost touch with his mother. His protector. All the emotions from before, adrenaline, anxiety, fear, anger, all came back to the front.

Jude collapsed onto the floor, rolling as he landed on his side. Bringing his hands up to his face, he hollered. Tears burned down his face as his hands balled into tight fists. He pulled his knees up to his chest, his whole body tense and scorching from exhaustion. His cries echoed around the room.

A gentle hand rested on Jude's shoulder. Jude jumped, hollering in fear and rolling to his other side, away from where the hand seemed to come from.

"Judas," came Jesus' reassuring voice. "My brother, it hurts me so to see you like this." Jude's hollers softened to grunts and whimpers as he attempted to hear Jesus. "I am so sorry," he continued. "I know what I did hurt you, has hurt you, and continues to. I know what I've done was horrendous."

Jude shot up off the floor, almost knocking Jesus over. "I watched you murder children," Jude lamented. "Those children were terrible, but you murdered them."

"I know…" Jesus replied.

"Thou shall not murder!" Jude yelled. "You claim to be a man of the law, that nothing of the law should change."

"And I stand by that," Jesus said.

"Then why?" Jude demanded.

Jesus chuckled.

"What's so funny?" Jude asked. "You think killing children is funny?"

"Excuse the laughter," Jesus asked. "It's uncomfortable enough to talk about, let alone justify it."

Jesus' head tilted up toward the light dangling from the ceiling. His eyes closed; it could've been the cover of any evangelical pamphlet. Except Jesus wasn't white.

"Well?" Jude demanded.

Lowering his head, Jesus' eyes opened and looked to his hands. A sly grin spread across his face. "It was mostly childhood ignorance," Jesus replied. "Your time has an issue with powerful weapons that, left to children, causes significant harm or damage."

"Guns," Jude replied.

"Guns…" Jesus repeated. "Powerful dangerous things when those that don't understand their potential play with them." Jude nodded. "The difference between them and myself," Jesus continued, "is that I can't have the weapon taken away from me. As children, we are constantly told we are at our most free. Free from responsibilities, from caring for others, from taxes… but do you remember feeling that way?"

Jude paused, his eyes focused, deep in thought. "It was a prison," Jude replied.

"Your home absolutely was," Jesus said. "You and your sister, alone with two people who may have loved you, but put their own pride before your emotional well-being."

Jude choked on the lump that leapt up in his throat.

"So when we get a taste of power," Jesus continued, "we use and abuse that power as often as we can. And when things don't go our way?" He gestured with a broad sweep of his arm to nothing in particular. "That power sometimes is all we have."

Jude didn't respond.

"Do you know why it was so easy for me to do it?" Jesus asked. Jude nodded. "Because of my powers," he continued. "I could see into, not just our own future, but multiple."

Raising an eyebrow, Jude's head cocked to the side. "What do you mean?" he asked.

"We live," Jesus started, holding his hand out, palm up, and from the ether appeared a bright yellow orb with several smaller orbs encircling it, "here." A small blue orb enlarged, the others dissipating into mist. It was Earth. "A small planet, around an average star," he continued. "That star is one of many billions of other stars, among billions of other galaxies, in this one *particular* universe. While our faith preaches a creation, *ex nihilo*, it's far more complex. From what your modern teachers and scientists call 'the Big Bang,' the process of the universe was set in a specific motion."

"And?" asked Jude.

"And," continued Jesus, "this universe isn't the only one."

Turning his head away, it was Jude's turn to laugh.

"You're not just a magician," Jude chuckled. "You're a lunatic too."

"You don't believe me," Jesus said.

"Why should I?" Jude exclaimed. "What reason do I have to believe you? You've got a seemingly unlimited supply of superpowers I can't get a grasp of, you go from predator to prophet, and now you're telling me the science fiction I enjoyed before coming to this hell hole is fact." Jude laughed and, without warning, collapsed into tears. "None of this makes sense," he wept.

"Please," Jesus said. "Let me try to explain."

10

"What is in my hand?" Jesus asked Jude.

Holding out his hand, palm up, Jesus nodded at it as Jude dried the tears from his cheek.

"Nothing," Jude sobbed.

Jesus chuckled.

"What?" Jude asked.

"I knew you would say that," Jesus said. "In fact, from a molecular level, what I am holding up is quite plentiful. Are you able to see these molecules?"

"No," Jude scoffed.

"I can," said Jesus, in a matter-of-fact fashion.

Jude gave him a blank stare. "I'm sorry," Jude asked, shaking his head. "You can see... oxygen?"

"I can see various elements," Jesus corrected. "I can see how they interact with one another; I can see a vibrant spectrum of chemical interactions. It might be comparable to musicians 'seeing' sound. A condition called synesthesia, or chromesthesia, might be comparable in your day."

Jude stared at him with a blank look. Nodding, Jesus looked up at Jude.

"It means that they see sound," Jesus explained. "Either music, or ordinary, everyday sounds carry some audible quality that makes their brain see colors in various patterns. That is similar to what I see."

After a moment, Jude cleared his throat. "So you just constantly see a rainbow everywhere?" Jude asked.

Jesus laughed. "No, my brother," he said. "While it is always there, it is not until I bring my attention specifically to it that I can see it and manipulate it."

Jude shook his head. "I'm sorry," he said. "Did you say manipulate it?"

"I did," said Jesus.

Another pregnant pause hung in the air.

"So what does that mean?" Jude asked, at last.

"You no doubt have heard of my ability to heal," Jesus said. "Long before you were brought here and adopted by my family."

"I have," Jude said.

"You also are aware of a concept called 'color-by-number?'" Jesus asked. "That is perhaps the closest I can come to explaining what it is like."

"So," Jude hesitated. "So… you connect particles like colors in a rainbow?"

Jesus bobbed his head from side to side, a reluctant smirk on his lips. "In so many words," he said. "But it's more. It's an energy. It… It's an emotion as well." His hands in front of him, as if clutching an invisible orb, shook up and down as he tried to find his words. Chuckling, Jesus dropped his hands between his legs, turning his head to Jude.

"Try explaining the color blue to a blind person," Jesus said. "It's like that. It's hard to explain something to someone who cannot experience it."

"How do you see it?" Jude asked.

"My father," Jesus said. "My real father is a man with extraordinary power. He was the one you saw; the one that killed the boy."

Jude blinked, unfazed.

"He has the ability to manipulate the fourth dimension," Jesus continued. "Time."

"So he's a time traveler," Jude said. He coughed out a laugh in disbelief.

"Why do you mock?" Jesus asked. "He's the reason you're here."

Jude's demeanor took a swift, and cold, shift. He brought his hands to his face, rubbing his eyes with clenched fists.

"That psychotic brat?" Jude asked.

"I cannot change who he is," Jesus said.

"That cretin," Jude interjected. "That monster that took me away from my life?"

"And what a life it was," Jesus stopped him, his face stern and intimidating. "What has my family given you? You are, and always have been, one of us."

Jude sobbed, holding back the intermittent gasps as he fought to focus on Jesus.

"Do not bite the hand that feeds you," Jesus warned.

Jude, locked in place, nodded in a frantic bob of his head.

"Now," Jesus continued, gesturing over to one side of the room they were in, "I have this shared ability with my father."

Jude turned his attention to where Jesus pointed. Realizing how small the room was, maybe no more than 16 to 18 feet long and wide, Jude jumped when he brought his gaze to the floor. A complete skeleton was laying on its side, jaw agape. It was surrounded by other skeletal pieces and fragments of skulls.

"That's me," Jesus said.

Jude whipped back around.

"Wait…" Jude started.

"This is a location in the southern United States," Jesus said. "Or what *was* the United States, several hundred years after a nuclear event that nearly wiped out the human population."

Jude shook his head.

"So how is your skeleton—" Jude began.

"I'm being used as an example," Jesus sighed. "My father is doing important work to ensure history continues as it should."

"So he..." Jude said. "...you... you could bring me home."

"No," Jesus said.

"W-what?" Jude became incredulous.

Jesus brought up a hand to stop Jude's protest. "I want to ask you to think about something," Jesus said. "Suppose you stayed in your present era, but were subjected to all the abuses you faced before."

A portal popped open next to them. Jude automatically recognized himself. He looked much the same, except he was sitting up against a fence. Jude recognized the spot. It was the gate by the train tracks about five miles from his parents' home, right near the convenience store his mother forbade him to enter. There were always homeless people there. And while he never saw it himself, the location had a reputation for prostitution and drug use. The portal revealed Jude to have longer hair with a ratty-looking beard. He was frail, thinner than he was now. Several dirty sweatshirts hung off his body, his jeans damp and tattered. The shoes on his feet, if one could call them that, reflected with duct tape on the toes. At first, Jude swore he was watching himself breathe into his hands for warmth. Then he noticed the light that kept flickering in and out of sight from his hands.

"Meth," Jesus said.

That's when Jude saw the open wounds on his hands and face.

"I don't understand," Jude said. "What am I looking at?"

"If my father had not come and taken you," Jesus said, "this was your fate."

"But I came from—" Jude started to say.

"You came from a war zone," Jesus interrupted. "Your leadership provided no opportunities for healing and care where you hurt the most." Jesus stood up, bringing himself over to Jude, he placed his head against his brother's. Jesus placed his hands around the back of Jude's neck, exhaling a soft cloud through his nose. "Your mind," he said. "You started with alcohol that friends brought into your schools. Then it was stealing cigarettes from your mother's purse. You would try marijuana, but you wouldn't like the feeling it gave you. Opioids, pain pills your doctor would prescribe you after an accident from drinking, would make you feel drowsy. You wouldn't like the vomiting that comes with it, and someone who would empathize with you, and wants your money, would offer you meth."

Jude looked down at his feet. He felt ashamed, and he hadn't even done the things Jesus described. Yet he knew, had things been different, those are exactly the things he would have done. "I hate this," Jude said. "I can't believe I did those things. I said I never would."

"But you didn't," Jesus said, embracing Jude.

Jude squeezed Jesus back, burrowing his face in his neck.

"That," began Jesus, "was another reality. Another timeline."

Pulling away, Jude rubbed his eyes. He sniffed back the mucus that started to drip from his nose, using the back of his arm to clear away any moisture. "An alternate dimension?" Jude asked.

"In a way," Jesus said. "Time moves like a river and, in some instances, breaks away into a separate timeline. In your case, you either are taken into the past, as that is what you are currently experiencing, or remain in your time and..." Jesus gestured at the open portal.

For a moment, Jude watched himself suckle at the end of the glass tube he was smoking out of. He was focused, but the look in his eyes made him sorrowful.

"I've heard about this," Jude spoke at last. "It was a sci-fi concept when I was a kid. The multi-verse theory, right?"

"Correct," Jesus said.

"So..." Jude sniffled. "There's an alternate time for each and every decision?"

"Not quite," Jesus corrected him. "Our universe, the one we occupy, is deterministic."

"I have no idea what that means," Jude said.

"It means," Jesus said, "that everything that does happen is supposed to happen. Once the universe started to expand, it did so because of how things on the microcosm of the universe, the quanta, affected the macrocosm. The cosmos, if you will."

"So," Jude said, "it's the tiny stuff that affects the bigger things?"

"Exactly," Jesus exclaimed. "Like individual grains of sand in a sand castle, how those move and stay together affects the structure that becomes your castle. And once that process is set in motion, everything else is determined to happen exactly as it does."

"And in my case?" Jude asked.

"There are only two opportunities for your timeline," Jesus said. "Either as my brother, my apostle, or..." He gestured toward the portal again. "There may be an ever-inflated number of timelines that start differently," Jesus continued. "Yet not all of them lead to the successful structure of the universe like you see it. Nor anything similar to it. So, most are never truly created. And of those possibilities that do exist, very little changes the course of events. The one that does is supernatural. It is one that literally requires divine intervention in order to create a new reality. In other words, in order for a different outcome to occur, nearly everything changes, molecularly, from the beginning. In some instances, that equates to no universe at all."

"So..." Jude asked, sounding unsure. "This is it?"

"It is," Jesus said. "You are where you are supposed to be because a deterministic universe brought you here."

Jude swallowed hard.

"I need to..." Jude stammered, "...be-betray you?"

"Those are the words of those who do not understand," Jesus reassured him. "Those are not my words."

"Then what are your words?" asked Jude.

"I say," Jesus concluded, "that you are doing what you are called to do."

"This is my purpose," Jude hung his head.

"Why do you fret, my brother?" Jesus asked.

"Because of who people think I am," Jude said. "What my name means... my reputation."

"And what would they say?" Jesus asked. "If you could use one word, and I will not accept betrayal, what is it you are labeled with? What fits your crime?"

Jude brought his hands to his face, coughing out short gasps and wet snorts. "E-Evil..." Jude gasped.

"My brother," Jesus cooed. He held out his hand. Within it appeared a dingy chalice, materialized out of nowhere. It was as if it had broken water tension and emerged from the ether. Jesus, turning to look behind him, located a bottled water.

"Hm..." Jesus said, analyzing the bottle.

"Is that...?" Jude began to ask.

"A plastic bottle from the era you were born into," Jesus said. "It was only present for a short time in your history. Replaced with more sustainable, and environmentally conscious, products shortly after the environmental reform around the year 2030 of your time." Jesus opened the bottle and started to pour the contents into the chalice. He shook his head while wearing a perturbed smirk. "It did little good," he said. "Too little, all too late. Arming hostile nations and helping to finance nuclear arsenals by the leader of your country, a decade prior, did little else but set the clock for humanity's end."

Handing the cup to Jude, Jesus waved his hand over the chalice. The water swirled with a red so dark, it almost appeared black. Jude looked up at Jesus, his jaw slacked. "Don't give me that look," Jesus joked. "I know you've heard *that* story."

Jude looked back down at the cup he held in his hands. With the aromatic, fruity scent of the wine, Jude felt a sudden sense of relief. His mind went to evenings sitting beside his mother as she read him the Lord of the Rings books before bed. She had spent her evenings reading, sipping Merlot, and giggling at grown up jokes in her Vonnegut books.

This was the time Jude would have her all to himself. His sister in bed, maybe his dad was home from work, maybe not. It was like a sacred space, the Holy Tabernacle of their house. Only select individuals were allowed in, and others could not desecrate it with their words or presence. It was the only signal Jude's dad ever noticed during arguments, and respected enough to give his mom space.

Jude brought the chalice to his lips and took a deep swig. The sharp bite of the wine, the gentle burn against his uvula as it slid down his throat, was like sensory time travel. His mother's red-tinted lips, the smell of her wine as she read from his books. She occasionally allowed Jude small sips of the wine, with the condition he never tell his father. He swore he could smell her perfume as well.

As he sipped more, Jude was equally as affected by another set of memories. Only the emotions were not the same. Jude recalled coming around the corner to his parents' bedroom, his father hunched over and sobbing. Then he saw him bring a wine bottle to his lips and chug. Jude would cautiously step up beside him. His father was not vulnerable like this around Jude's mother, and it was rare to see him display any emotion that was not serious. Or, in most cases, angry. Each time Jude found his father like this, he would become embarrassed. He would struggle to dry his tears, hide the bottle, and act like everything was fine.

Jude always waited for his father to initiate the next step. It was usually a "Hey buddy," or some other attempt at giving him a playful pet name and offset their discomfort. It didn't ever last more than a moment. He would apologize to Jude for... everything. Jude never felt he understood what was going on, why Mom and Dad were so angry at each other. Mom ignored it, but his dad always explained things in a way Jude understood. Or at least what he needed to know. And he always hugged him. He always professed his commitment to doing everything he could so his sister and he could end up with better lives. He told Jude he loved him.

"You know what you are to me?" his dad would whisper to him, tears streaking down his face.

"What?" Jude would ask, a hopeful smile on his face. The routine his father started, their expression of love for each other, always made him beam.

"You're the particles in the space around me," he would start. "The air in my lungs, the photons from the sun, the earth I walk upon..."

"...You're my only one," Jude would finish.

His father would hug him tight, kiss him on the forehead, and then look back over his shoulder. "Don't tell your mother," he would say, winking at Jude as he pulled the bottle out.

"Judas?" asked Jesus.

Jude's eyes snapped open, blinking in rapid succession as he looked up and back to his glass of wine. Guzzling down the remainder, Jesus held out the water bottle to offer more to Jude. Holding out the chalice, Jude offered his gratitude as Jesus filled the cup.

"You are not evil," Jesus said after a pause. "And what you are being asked to do is not evil."

Jesus gently pushed from the bottom of the chalice until it reached Jude's lips. Jude tilted his head back, the red wine drizzling down the side of his face, staining his cheek. Jesus snickered, rubbing the wine off his face with the sleeve of his robe. Starting to feel a buzz again, Jude cackled as he held his arm up over his face. Wine dripped from his elbow. Guiding Jude to the other side of the room, Jesus waved his arm to reveal another portal. This one showed the outside of an apartment, placed above what appeared to be a brewery at night. A single light shone through one window. Jesus gestured toward the portal.

11

Stepping through the portal, Jude's feet landed on a gravel roadway. The smell was of fermentation, hops, and barley, the scents he became familiar with when his father had friends over who brewed their own beers. The sound of machinery, pistons discharging, metal clanking together filled the soundscape.

As Jude sipped his wine, there was something in the mix of noises that caught his attention. A different frequency. Arhythmic patterns. No discernible repetition, save for the type of noise. For a brief moment, the louder machines quieted. Voices started hollering, a clambering for something. Perhaps a tool. Perhaps they were disciplining someone. Even with the addition of the voices, Jude still heard something.

Screaming.

A hand grabbed around the middle of his bicep, making him jump.

"Shhhh," Jesus hissed. "It's only me."

"Someone's being hurt," Jude said, attempting to walk toward the building.

"Wait," Jesus said. His eyes glowed with a faint white light, and the sounds around them stopped. No justification. No cries of surprise or anger. Just nothing.

Jude rubbed his fingers over his ears, shaking his head and looking around with a horrified look on his face. Snapping his fingers next to his ears, spinning around, and grabbing Jesus, Jude pulled him close. "What happened?" Jude demanded. "Why can't I hear anything? What did you do?"

"You can't hear anything when sound waves aren't travelling to you," Jesus said, smiling.

Jude turned slowly, spotting several dots of light in the space around them. As he crept toward them, he saw lightning bugs. Their tails were lit, wings spread out, like immortalized statutes to unappreciated beauty.

"You stop time?" Jude asked.

"You've seen me do it before," Jesus said.

"Just once," Jude replied. "When we were kids." Placing his hands around the firefly, Jude felt a warm vibration, and a sound like the low notes on the piano. "Incredible," Jude whispered.

"Come," Jesus said. "I have much to show you."

Jesus walked through a door, leading into a stairwell. At the second level, Jesus walked down the empty halls. A door appeared every few feet, the walls brown with faded red doors. Scuffs from years of furniture being moved in and out of the building littered the walls, dents and missing chunks of door or paneling speckled about the scene. Jesus stopped at a door and opened it, looking behind himself at Jude.

The apartment they entered was modest. It appeared dishes were in progress in the sink from dinner, and a newspaper, with a language Jude couldn't read, sat on a worn out sofa in an attached room.

"Here," Jesus said.

Jude turned his attention down the hallway from the kitchen. Jesus stood outside a room where a light was illuminating the hallway. Just beside the door stood a young woman in a tulip bell skirt, her head hung down, hands folded over her stomach. "Who is—" Jude started to ask, pointing at the woman.

"No," Jesus stopped him, pointing into the room. "This is what I need you to see."

Approaching the room, Jude looked at the woman's face. Frail-looking, with dark brown hair, her face stretched into a scowl; she looked as if she were fighting from crying out. It was like Jude expected her to fall over into a trembling heap, bellowing as she fell.

As Jude looked into the room, he jumped back with a yelp. Before him stood a mountain of a man; he was barrel-chested, with a grey head of hair that looked more appropriate for the military range than a brewery. Sporting a long, handle-bar style mustache, he was older and dressed the part. His black slacks were held up by suspenders, with a white t-shirt underneath, and loafers on his feet. It was like gazing at a violent caricature of his own grandfather. With one arm held up high, balled into a fist, it was what was in his other hand that startled Jude the most.

A child.

The boy, no more than eight or nine, clutched the man's wrist with one hand, a wrist that was attached to a hand that gripped the boy by the collar. He appeared to dangle from the man's hand. The boy's other hand was extended out toward the raised fist. His face was covered in bruises, one eye swollen shut, blood gushing from his nose. Fear was the only thing Jude could find in the eye that could still be seen. And the monster of a man hulking over him had veins bulging from his neck and temple, his arms looking as if they might burst open from the tension of his own muscles. He looked to be hollering something at the boy.

"What does this look like to you?" Jesus asked.

Jude didn't answer.

"Jude?" Jesus called.

"Hm?" Jude replied.

"What does this look like?"

"Fuck…" Jude exhaled. "That man is beating this poor kid."

Taking a step toward them, Jesus hollered to Jude. "No!" he pleaded. "You cannot interact with them."

"We need to stop this," Jude said. "Don't we need to stop this? Don't we…?"

"No," Jesus shook his head. "Remember how I told you there was only one alternate timeline? One that required divine intervention?"

"Yes," Jude replied.

"We are the interveners here," Jesus explained. "I'm not telling you these things because we physically cannot, but we should not. We would create a new branch of time by changing what happens here. It would make our whole journey more difficult in attempting to find our way back home. My father said it would be like trying to find a path out of a corn maze in the dark."

Jude pulled back, analyzing the situation again. "So there's nothing—" Jude started.

"Out of the question," replied Jesus. "Please answer the question I asked you."

Jude took another gulp of his wine, shaking the chalice with his arm extended. After a second, the cup became more weighted, and Jude returned it to his lips. "This is fucked up," he said. "You're asking me to stand here and watch some massive brute beat this child? Who knows what damage has been done already? There was something they had when I was a kid..." He took another sip from his cup. "They were called to my home a couple times," he continued. "My sister and I were crying while my parents fought." Jude's foot tapped with a feverish rhythm against the floor, as if motorized. "Do they have an agency like that here?" he asked. "Can we let them know?"

"No," Jesus stated. "We are not here to intervene. We are here so you can learn about the nature of evil. So you can see why your role is significant, and why it is far from evil."

Taking another sip of wine, Jude massaged the bridge of his nose. "Well," he said, "I've already told you what it looks like. I can't imagine this is some trick where it turns out he's playing a game and they're having a wonderful time together."

"You're correct," Jesus said. "The man is unfairly assaulting a child. Not just any child, but the first of his four children with his wife that lived."

"Fuck..." said Jude.

"One would think," Jesus began, "given how precious this man likely knows life is, he would be reluctant to cause harm to his child."

"My parents never even spanked me," Jude chimed in.

"Yet you bear the internal scars of abuse," Jesus clarified.

Jude didn't respond.

"A military man," Jesus continued. "He had two wives prior to the woman out there. Both died from natural causes. He's a civil servant, believe it or not. A lot of his personal belongings disappeared when he found a farm too difficult to manage, and the economic difficulties would later bring his people, and his country, to war. And this is what happened to him…"

Jesus wove his hand in front of him, and the entire environment changed. Back on a rocky road, in broad daylight, they were in front of what appeared to be a bar. Everything moved as it should. Jude ducked behind a barrel to not be seen by a group of children playing up the path.

"Relax," Jesus insisted, pointing at the ground. Jude looked down to notice a large oval that encircled him. There was a similar shape under Jesus. Within that circle was the flooring of the prison cell. "Bubbles," Jesus said. "We're witnessing this from the privacy of the cell, but we are witnessing the moment as if we are there."

Jude, with reluctant steps, moved back toward Jesus. He stared down at his feet as he rejoined him.

"Look," Jesus said, pointing in the doorway of a bar. The hulking man they saw before was seated on a stool at the bar, a glass in front of him. A man behind the bar reached out, stating something Jude couldn't understand, with a newspaper in his hand. With a sudden jerk, the behemoth flopped to the ground like a rag doll. Other men, unseen until they came to the man's aid, rushed to his side. Some slapped his face, one stepped outside the bar and shouted to the group of children playing a few feet away. All of them ran up the road toward the other buildings.

"So he died of a heart attack," Jude said. "The only surprising thing is he had a heart that could give out."

"Stroke," Jesus corrected him. "He's already dead, but that's not what I wanted you to see."

A few of the children from before came sprinting back. This time, an older child, perhaps in his early teens, came running with them. Squinting, Jude looked back at the children.

"Is that...?" Jude asked.

"The boy from before," Jesus said. "Watch him."

With a panicked look in his eyes, Jude swore it was the same look he'd given before as the corpse that lay before him beat him within an inch of his life. As the boy peered into the bar, just in time to observe the men lifting and carrying off the man, he dropped to his knees and burst into tears. The children came up to him, all embracing him as he shook with sobs.

"He was a monster," Jude said. "Why would he be sorrowful about him dying?"

"Do you think people deserve death?" Jesus asked.

Jude looked down at the children, his brow furrowed and tense.

"Depends," Jude said.

"On what?" asked Jesus.

"Would the abuse have continued?" Jude demanded. "Would he have persisted in beating that boy?"

"Of the man's older children," Jesus said, "aside from the boy here, there were two older children. One of them, an older brother, left home because of the abuse."

"Good," Jude said.

"So what of the younger siblings?" Jesus continued. "Do they deserve to be left in a home where abuse is rampant? Where, in their formative years, they are shown nothing but harsh treatment from someone considered the head of household?"

Jude paused a moment.

"Shouldn't someone aware of the situation," Jesus continued, "do everything in their power to alleviate others from their suffering?"

"No," Jude said

Jesus cocked his head to the side. "Why do you say that?" asked Jesus.

"Because," Jude started, swallowing back the pain that manifested in his throat. "Because sometimes when you are removed from the situation, you only have the energy to watch out for yourself."

Jesus hummed and nodded. Jude continued to watch the children, now rubbing the poor boy's back and speaking softly to him.

"Go on," Jesus said.

"Look," Jude exclaimed. "You're right. My home was terrible. My parents' anger and aggression toward one another was painful. Why couldn't they get along? Why couldn't they love each other like I loved them? Why wasn't what I did enough?" Jude slid the back of his sleeve across his face. "And my sister..." he started.

"Did they not treat you with love?" Jesus asked.

Jude stopped and gripped at the sides of his robe. He shuffled the fabric back and forth between his fingers. "They did," Jude muttered, biting his lip. "But only when the fighting stopped. Only when they noticed I was in the room."

"Are your parents evil?" Jesus pressed.

Jude shook his head, pursing his lips.

"Even though they've caused such harm to you?" Jesus inquired.

"Never," Jude said. "I couldn't feel as close to them as I did when we had our private moments."

Jesus nodded, silent at first.

"People manage trauma differently," Jesus explained. "Even our sweet child here."

Waving his arm again, Jude found they had been moved to a bathroom area. An older man wearing a bow tie, slicked back salt-and-pepper hair, and a stethoscope in his ears. He was listening to the heart rate of a woman sitting in the bathtub. Another man, seated behind the woman in the tub, was rubbing a sponge that left a yellowish streak across the woman's skin. He frequently picked up a small jar, dabbing the sponge inside.

The man listening to the woman's heart shook his head, removing the stethoscope from his ears and gently placing them back in his black bag beside the bathtub. With a noticeable reluctance, the man began to speak. A stutter at first, he sighed with a defeated sound and began to say something to the two others present.

Jesus' hand came out and, as if turning a globe, the room moved until Jude and Jesus found themselves behind the doctor, looking at the other person in the room. It was the boy, all grown up now. His mother was the one seated in the bath tub; she had dark, bruised scarring around her chest. Her breasts gone. She looked much more frail than before. The boy breathed with hesitation as he sat over her.

As the doctor enunciated his message, the tears started to surge down the boy's face. He buried his face into the nape of his mother's neck, pulling her close to him. With the fortitude of a mountain, his mother remained stoic. Placing her hand on his arm, her index finger stroked his skin with a tenderness, terrified of breaking him.

Without looking up at them, the doctor turned, picked up his bag, and exited the apartment. The boy wailed into his mother's neck. She shushed him, closing her eyes. Mumbling something soft to him, her hand moved to his head. Combing her fingers through her hair, spinning small locks between the tips of her fingers, Jude felt his heart sink.

"She's dying," Jude said.

"By morning," Jesus said.

Despite the significant sorrow felt in his gut, despite his desire to offer consolation, to say "I lost my mother too," no tears came to Jude's eyes. Instead, he marveled at the strength held by this woman. Her battle was so much more than physical, the ailments of the cancer. The wounds she bore on the surface were mere scratches compared to what was raging inside her. The despair Jude felt, seeing his mother's tears hit the page as she read to him at night, was all too familiar to what he felt now. As then, Jude remained phlegmatic. His eyes dry, his chin up, he carried this for himself so the women, so important yet so abused, wouldn't bear any more.

"How would you describe this boy?" Jesus asked. Waving his hand once again, they found themselves in an art studio. The boy, now appearing to be in his twenties, sat at a canvas. With precision required of a marksman, the boy glided the brush in small, dotted strokes.

"Is this all his work," Jude asked, glancing around the room. Several other canvases, some completed, some with holes punched in them from assumed failed attempts, sat stacked against one another. A few dozen blank canvases sat beside him, otherwise. Most of the pictures were of scenery, full of lavish detail. The colors were vibrant, and looked almost like a photograph.

"It is," said Jesus. "So what do you think of him?"

With an impressed smile, Jude nodded as he examined the artwork.

"The man's got talent," Jude said. "Isn't that where all true artistry comes from? Suffering and loss?"

"Is this man evil?" Jesus asked.

"Absolutely not!" Jude exclaimed. "He's suffered undeservedly. This is like the story of Job."

"Interesting," said Jesus.

"Think about it," Jude continued. "Job loses everything material and invaluable to him. His home, his livestock, his wealth, and, the real meat of the problem, his family."

"That almost sounds like the boy's father," said Jesus.

"That son of a bitch didn't have the right to take out his losses on his child like that," Jude snapped.

"So this man?" Jesus asked. "You think he is good?"

"I have no reason to think otherwise," said Jude.

"Job was good," Jesus said.

"Yeah," Jude said through gritted teeth. "Because God decided to play a game with Satan to test his faith."

"He gave him everything back," said Jesus. "That makes it fair, doesn't it?"

"All things being equal," said Jude, "no."

"Why?" asked Jesus.

"If it were just his house," said Jude, "his belongings, his money… no!" Jude threw his hands up in the air, pacing in a circle. "No, it's not fair," he continued. "When we don't have money, you and I, we cannot afford the things we need. Simon can't fish because he can't pay the taxes. We can't pay our tribute to the Temple. I hear they're going to start taxing us simply for being Jews! You know what happens when we can't pay our taxes; you've seen them make our neighbors an example for the rest of the village. And when—"

Jesus pointed at Jude's cup. Jude, as if by instinct, jerked his arm up. Holding the cup just under Jesus' chin, Jesus placed his hand over the cup and the red wine bubbled up to the brim. With a gentle bend of his arm, Jude sipped from the chalice for a moment. With a loud swallow, he sighed and re-centered himself.

"I am just so sick of the Romans…" Jude started to speak.

"I know," said Jesus. "Their time is coming."

Jude sipped at his wine, savoring the sensations and pleasant memories of his time with his mother. The burn in his stomach reminded him of his father's hug, and the warm vibrato of his voice.

"He's good," Jesus said. "Objectively?"

Jude sighed, squinting his eyes. "I'm sure he's not," Jude said. "Next you're going to tell me he ground up his mother and used her paste to paint his pictures."

Jesus smirked.

"This man eventually found great success," Jesus said. "He became a very powerful politician. He had a pet dog he loved and was a vegetarian."

"Politician?" asked Jude, surprised. "He didn't go to art school?"

"He tried," said Jesus. "He never actually made it in."

"Well," scoffed Jude. "That speaks for his natural talent."

"He had another talent," said Jesus. "One that outshined his other skills."

"Of course he did," Jude said. "What was it?"

"He was an excellent orator," Jesus replied. "He had a way of getting people worked up."

"So he gave speeches," Jude said. "I'm dying to know who this is. Any speeches I might know?"

Jesus, looking to Jude out of the corner of his eye, snapped his fingers. Jude realized he was in a crowd, shouting rabidly in a language he didn't understand. Before them, on a platform with numerous flags, was a podium with several microphones attached. Behind the podium was the boy. A full-grown man, his dark hair was slicked to the side, a unique mustache on his lip. The poor, sad empath had long since gone. His eyes read with greed, excitement, and arousal.

That's when Jude saw the red arm band. And heard the chants...

Sieg heil! Sieg heil! Sieg heil!

12

"What the fuck!" hollered Jude, throwing the chalice. The scenery around them dissipated, revealing the brick cell they had been in before. The chalice smashed against the brick wall and scattered among the skeletal remains. "What the actual fuck?!" Jude flailed his arms around as he paced through the cell.

"Judas," Jesus pleaded with him, chuckling as he patted his back.

"What kind of mind fuck are you trying to put me through?" Jude shouted at Jesus. "Do you think, after everything I went through, you want me having the weight of *empathizing* with that piece of shit?"

"My brother," Jesus called. "I meant no ill will."

Jude knocked on the sides of his head with the base of his hands. "Out! Out! Out!" he hollered, ruffling his hands through his hair. "I can't stop!"

"It's the cognitive dissonance of evil," Jesus explained. "Not just in this instance, but people who do commit evil often come from backgrounds rife with trauma and abuse." Jude breathed deep, fast breaths. He wheezed with each exhale. "Relax," Jesus said, keeping a straight face. "You are safe here. You are protected."

Jesus rubbed Jude's shoulder. As tense as he was, as furious as he felt, there was always something about his family's touch that soothed Jude. It never made it go away, but it made it bearable.

"I-I-" Jude stuttered. "I'm okay, brother."

"Good people are capable of terrible things," Jesus reassured him.

Jude lurched forward, retching onto the floor. Jesus wrapped his arms around him, struggling to hold him up. Opening his eyes, feeling the next wave of nausea hit him, Jude discovered a small portal was open below him. Traces of his vomit littered around the outside of the portal. Within it, however, was a sight that took Jude's breath away. An object, like a star, shone a distance away. Unlike a star, the light formed rings around a silhouette. Like a phantom version of Saturn, save for the arch of light formed over the dome of the silhouette.

Jude's heart quickened; he felt the bile rise in the back of his throat. Arching his back, he felt as if his neck were stretching like a cartoon. The light red, almost Kool-Aid colored, liquid erupted from his mouth, quickly disappearing into the void below him.

The hole closed, and Jesus pulled Jude back into a seated position. Through wet gasps, mucus and saliva dangling down his face like a discarded spider web, Jude reassured Jesus.

"I'm okay..." Jude said. "I'm okay."

Jesus held up his hand and the scattered remains of the chalice rose up from out of the bones and snapped into his hand. Whole. As if nothing had happened. Whirling his finger, water appeared in the cup, and Jesus handed it to Jude.

"I'll let that stay as water," Jesus chuckled. "I'm sorry my brother. I knew it was risky, but I also knew it would send the message home for you."

Jude swirled the water around in his mouth, spitting it off to the side.

"Are you saying Hitler was a good man?" Jude asked.

Again, Jesus laughed.

"You're asking me," Jesus choked back another laugh. "You're asking if I think a man who espoused racial superiority, who ordered the building and operation of death camps, and found economic security through forced labor, torture, and actual death is good?"

Jesus held up his hand and another, similar-looking, chalice appeared. Red wine appeared, ex nihilo, filled to the brim, and he took a long sip. Tilting his head back, his Adam's apple bobbed up and down as he gulped the wine. With a light, wet gurgle in his sternum, Jesus let out a relaxed tittle. "Not in the slightest," he said, bringing his head down to take another sip of wine.

"What's your reason?" Jude asked. "What was the point?"

Taking another sip of wine, Jesus looked up toward the ceiling. "Have you ever knowingly done something you shouldn't?" Jesus asked.

"That sounds like the Christian, 'have you ever told a lie' argument," Jude scoffed.

"I'm not looking to trap you," Jesus said, raising his glass to him. "It's an honest question."

Jude's eyes went to the upper left part of his skull, digging for an answer. "Once," he said. "When I was in school, we had a science test. I studied, but I never understood a lot of it. Mom and Dad promised me a new game if I got a B in the class."

"You felt pressured," Jesus said.

"The prospect of a new adventure," Jude clarified. "I was so sick of playing the same game over and over. I couldn't do anything else to distract me when my parents fought. I also hated how stupid I felt when I tried hard and they said I could do better."

"Pressure," Jesus restated.

"Yeah," Jude sighed. "Anyway, our desks had these frames around them, and our school let us carry all our books in our bags. Well, my science folder with my study guide was poking out. I laid my head on my desk, as I often did during these tests when I got frustrated, and with my left hand slid the paper out far enough to get the answers I needed."

"How did you do?" Jesus asked.

"I got a perfect score," Jude sighed. He sipped his water, turning to Jesus. "I've never told anyone that before," Jude said. "I was so ashamed."

"Was that the only time?" Jesus asked.

"That I did that?" Jude replied. "No. It was actually a few weeks later, same class. Even though I studied hard, again, I couldn't remember anything."

"And how did you do on that test?" Jesus asked.

"I got an 80," Jude said. "Out of 100."

"Not a perfect score," Jesus said. "Why?"

"I'm not a smart guy," Jude said. "They would have caught on."

"Judging by what you said before," Jesus said, "would it be safe to assume you were never caught?"

Jude chuckled. "No," he said. "There's lots of other stuff I've done that's worse."

"This example is perfect," Jesus said. "Did you ever cheat in your studies again after that?"

"No," Jude said. "I started hearing in classes about a friend's brother who cheated on a test during his first year at university. He failed and was expelled from his school. No school wanted him after that."

"Imagine that," Jesus said. "A person makes a mistake, and a harmless one at that, and they are shunned from academia. In your time, how difficult does life become if you cannot get an education?"

Jude shrugged.

"I heard stories about janitors working in schools 'cause they couldn't make it," Jude said. "Or my mom would point out trash collectors and construction workers who had to do dirty jobs. She would always say, 'Remember, you can do better.'"

"What's wrong with doing those things?" Jesus asked. "We need people to remove waste from our living spaces for health, for well-being. We need people to work on our roads, as our neighbors do in Nazareth, so that traveling is easy. So when things happen, our bridges are sturdy, our roads smooth, and people can find their way."

Jude thought for a moment, a single eyebrow raised. "Wow..." he thought.

"Think of that reputation, though," Jesus said. "Even though there is nothing wrong with the job, clearly people in your community felt it was beneath them."

"Absolutely," Jude agreed.

"Would it be safe to say," Jesus asked, "that perhaps this young man felt that reputation? Feared those job prospects more than being caught cheating? Perhaps he felt there was no way but through these means, as you felt for yours."

With a pregnant pause, Jude sipped at his water.

"I always felt like I was better than that guy," Jude said. "At least after that story."

"Why?" Jesus asked. "You both did something you admit is, to some degree, evil."

"Y-yes..." Jude stammered, as if having an epiphany mid-sentence. "It's actually because of that reason I felt better than him."

"Why?"

"Because," Jude paused, licking his lips. "Initially it was because I wasn't in college and he was. I couldn't get kicked out of school for cheating, so it didn't matter. And college is something you're paying money for so..."

"So he made an irresponsible choice," Jesus concluded. "He forfeited the thousands of dollars for an education he had just spent. He knew, or should have known, what was going to happen."

"Exactly!" Jude affirmed.

"Let me see if I have this straight," Jesus said. "In both your circumstance and his, there is an understanding that cheating in academia is wrong. Correct?"

"Yes," said Jude.

"Both of you faced some type of negative circumstance if you were unsuccessful," Jesus said. "Correct?"

"Of course," Jude responded.

"Knowing it was wrong, knowing what might happen, you both cheat," Jesus said. "The only difference is, somehow, one of you gets caught. Not only that, the one who is not caught is successful in cheating again."

Jude blinked, opening his mouth to respond. Nothing came.

"Cheating in academia is wrong for what reasons?" Jesus asked.

"It's dishonest," Jude replied, snapping to.

"Is that it?" Jesus asked.

"Well, no," Jude said. "We find truth through honest study and reporting. Like the autism thing."

"What happened there?" Jesus asked.

"Some guy," Jude continued, "he wrote a phony academic paper that said autism was linked to vaccines. A lot of people thought it was real, so people stopped giving their kids shots. I'm pretty sure that's why my friend Jake and I stopped hanging out as kids. Mom said they had different beliefs about medicine and it was best to find new friends who wouldn't make us sick."

"I wish that rumor had stopped in your time," Jesus said.

"I don't even understand why people gave a shit," Jude confessed. "I knew kids with autism and they were awesome. They knew the coolest stuff, and always had the hidden info on the games I liked. They were the only ones who could see when I had bad days. They never forced me to hug; they just liked to make sure I was okay."

"Sometimes it's those that suffer the most that offer the greatest compassion when we need it," Jesus said.

"Asshole scientist," Jude said. "And for what? He got caught and was basically black listed from scientific research. More interested in lining his pockets than helping people."

"Let me ask," Jesus said. "Were you able to run before you could walk?"

Jude scoffed. "Of course not."

"Maybe that's another way to see it," Jesus replied. "You can't skip steps while learning, otherwise you'll never be able to move onto the next phase of learning."

"Yeah but I tried," Jude decried. "I stared at those pages and couldn't remember a damn thing. All I *felt* was frustration, anxiety, depression, and idiocy."

"Not everyone's mind works the same," Jesus said. "This isn't a question of your intelligence. Another well-known Jew made an argument that, 'if you judge a fish by its ability to climb a tree, it will live its whole life believing that it is stupid.'"

"But what I did was wrong," Jude nodded.

"Should that moment define your life?" Jesus asked.

"No," Jude said. "Of course not."

"It certainly made that man's life more difficult," said Jesus. "But should his life be defined by that moment?"

"No," Jude said.

"But it's likely that it will," Jesus continued. "He may find employment, or another opportunity for education, but the struggle will lead to an indelible mark on him."

"I can see that," Jude said.

"You both had a lot to lose," Jesus said. "But the chance was still taken, not because you didn't know it was wrong, but because you didn't think you'd get caught."

Jude nodded.

"There was a greater goal," Jesus continued. "You both determined to take a risk in order to avoid negative consequences."

"Yes," Jude said.

"What about drug users?" Jesus asked.

"What about them?" Jude replied.

"Are they viewed favorably?"

"No," Jude insisted. "They…" He thought for a moment. "They knew what they were doing…" Jude trailed off. Glancing down at his glass, he wished for wine.

"The first time someone tries a drug," Jesus said, "that is when they might have a choice, in most cases. Afterwards, it's experimental, as most substance use is."

Looking down at Jude's cup, Jesus waved his hand and the water turned a dark red. Jude immediately downed the cup.

"Some people feel normal while on drugs," Jesus continued. "It silences intrusive thoughts; it provides a more immersive distraction from whatever is challenging them. And in some cases…" Jesus finished his wine. "…it is in order to not suffer. To avoid how their body feels without the drug."

Jude recalled days where he would tremble, involuntarily. Until the wine was in his body, his tremors made most things difficult to accomplish. Even walking.

"What does this have to do with Hitler?" Jude asked.

"Evil is not a black and white issue," Jesus said. "People in Germany, at the time of Hitler, viewed what he was doing as a great success for their country. Rampant anti-Semitism let people ignore the humanitarian rights being violated, that they knew about. They were otherwise kept in the dark about the death camps, and all messages broadcast on their televisions were controlled by those who didn't want anyone questioning Hitler's power."

Jude attempted to drain the remnants in his glass into his mouth.

"Let me show you something else," Jesus said, standing up. Jude followed suit, and the room around them disappeared. They found themselves in a large, open room. Small cots, barely registering as a place mat, were lined up down the room, in several rows. On the mats were emaciated, shriveled, shells of human beings. All had shaved heads and filthy rags and linen strewn about their respective spaces. Mixed between toddlers, children, and full-grown adults, the smell of feces, vomit, and urine burned in their nostrils. Women in white garments, nuns, walked up and down the aisles of children. Every once in a while, they may have bent over to check one of the patients. Otherwise, they smiled and continued to weave through the maze of corpses in waiting.

"What is this?" Jude asked.

"A hospital," Jesus said. "More importantly, a hospice."

"I get that they're dying," Jude said. "Is anyone... helping them?"

"Not to the extent that is necessary," said Jesus. "But yes."

"This is horrendous," Jude said. "And this is a hospital. Who runs this?"

"Mother Theresa," Jesus replied with no hesitation.

"Wait," Jude interjected. "Wait, wait, wait... This is run by Mother Theresa?"

"It is," Jesus replied.

"The Catholic holy woman from Calcutta?" Jude asked.

"Yes."

"There's absolutely no way—" Jude continued.

"Mother Theresa had questionable connections," Jesus quipped. "Questionable financial decisions. And this is the result of a general lack of care and consideration for human life. A woman who espoused generally anti-female views and disparaged reproductive rights. This is because she felt my suffering on the cross brought us all closer to God. She felt that suffering was next to godliness, like some second century martyr."

Jude looked around in abject horror. "This is disgraceful," he confessed.

And with a snap of his fingers, Jesus brought them back to the brick cell. "Good or evil?" Jesus asked.

"Mother Theresa?" Jude replied.

Jesus nodded.

"Uh..." Jude's back arched, scratching his neck. "I-I don't know."

"Come on, Judas," Jesus pleaded with him. "We feel guilt for acknowledging she did terrible things. Why do we feel guilty?"

"Because…" Jude thought for a moment. "She's Mother Theresa. She's not just a… sister? Is that what women priests are?"

"Yes," replied Jesus.

"There's something about the name," Jude continued. "Something about the word 'mother' being in her title. It feels… wrong to question her."

"Who would question their own mother?" Jesus asked. "Who would contradict her? Nobody questions priests, men we call 'Father,' because men have always dominated the public sphere. And church is a public gathering that treats everyone like family. In our homes, however, mother knows best."

"Wait—" Jude attempted to interject.

"Men grow up with problematic relationships to their mothers," Jesus continued. "They're submissive and docile, overcompensating for something they were criticized for as a child, or they're uncomfortably lovey with them."

"Isn't that being a little harsh?" Jude asked.

"Please," Jesus held up his hand. "Your country provides no maternity, *or* paternity, leave. Condoms can be bought over the counter while women need prescriptions from doctors and, sometimes, judgement and denial of services because of people's personal beliefs." Jesus huffed, placing his hands on his waist. "I don't ever remember telling people they can't take their medicine," Jesus snarled.

Jude looked Jesus up and down with cautious examination. "This bothers you," Jude said. "A lot."

Standing with clenched fists, Jesus bit the inside of his lip. "You've heard of the Crusades?" Jesus asked.

"Hard to avoid it where I grew up," Jude said.

"Horrendous war waged for petty reasons," Jesus said. "All carried out in my name. Your nation would eventually wage a war on the same regions already terrorized by western imperialists for centuries before. And your leader will use the word 'Crusade' as if it were something noble."

Jude nodded. "I wouldn't put it past my nation to do that," he said.

"Am I responsible for those things?" Jesus said. "Does the blood of all those slaughtered belong on my hands? The man who eventually sentenced me to death, who hates our people and kills them mercilessly until Rome removes him and the high priest long after I'm dead? *He* received sainthood. He gets held in high esteem. Meanwhile, your world depicts me in a state where I was hung in humiliation. I was a stain on the Roman effort to subjugate our people. I'm remembered as others might be with a noose or a firearm."

"Yeah," Jude hung his head.

"This is not your doing," Jesus reassured him. "Do not feel the guilt for something you did not create."

"Would you describe that as good?" Jude asked.

"Bumps in the road," Jesus said. "As much as I resent my name, my ministry, for being used for such terrors, it was used for good as well.

The room fell away in slow, almost liquid droplets. As it did, a room with an elongated table, stained to appear a dark amber color, appeared. A beet-red carpet with gold fringe lay beneath it. The chairs, an almost cream-colored fabric that was finely attended to, sat dozens of men in black robes. Some were adorned with red sashes, like waterfalls over both shoulders. Voices murmured, echoing off the paste-colored walls, the only decoration being a border that appeared to depict the Stations of the Cross.

Silence fell over the room as a door, behind the head of the table, emitted a loud thudding noise. Each person stood up, flattening their robes, turning their attention toward the opening doors. In walked an older gentleman, perhaps in his early fifties judging by the mix of brown and gray hair in his beard. A beard that dangled an inch or two over his chest. He sported some type of dark fabric helmet over his head, a circular piece of fabric over his shoulders matched. Sitting at the seat at the head of the table, one looking like a throne, one of the men seated next to him placed finely decorated papers in front of him.

"What am I watching?" asked Jude.

"This is Pope Gregory XIII," Jesus said. "The world was using the Julian calendar, and it wasn't working. The Earth did not spin exactly 365.25 days every year. They had a leap year every four years to compensate, but it wasn't working."

"What do you mean it wasn't working?" Jude asked.

"It's based on a solar calendar," said Jesus. "Society functioned for eons based on the weather, but it wasn't perfect. The Julian calendar was helpful, but something was still off. They were finding that days that were typically warmer were treading into snowy territory, and vice versa. It's not good for farmers, for those who provide food for themselves or others, who have to grow and harvest crops, raise animals, and slaughter them. Things that require having a good-faith knowledge of the calendar, were suddenly more difficult."

"So what happened?" Jude asked.

Jesus smiled. "It will not surprise you that it was not changed for any of those reasons," he admitted.

"Of course not," snickered Jude.

"They couldn't account for Easter with any certainty," Jesus said. Silence.

"You're joking," insisted Jude.

"Even more interesting," Jesus continued. "It was to distance Easter from Passover."

"Wait…" said Jude. "You mean, the historically significant holiday where you were executed while in the midst of celebrating?"

"The same," Jesus confirmed.

"That's terrible," Jude scowled. "Why would that be a good thing?"

"Regardless of the motives," Jesus said, "it produced a lot of good. It wasn't universally adopted at first, or really at all. Average citizens thought it was a scheme to cheat them out of half a month's rent. That was because, at that point, the poor dating of the Julian calendar had set them back almost that much time. The proposal to cut out so many days would decimate some families financially, as they would then be expected to come up with a full month's rent in half the time."

"Wow," said Jude, shaking his head.

"It took several hundred years to have it adopted globally," said Jesus.

"All because they didn't want to mix up Easter and Passover," Jude said.

"So," asked Jesus. "Good or evil?"

13

"What do you mean?" asked Jude.

"Was the adoption of the Gregorian calendar an act of good, or evil?" Jesus responded.

"I don't see how that—" Jude started.

"Was there benefit or loss?" Jesus asked.

"Well, loss, I guess, for the people who couldn't afford rent," Jude replied. "I mean, unless they had an understanding landlord."

"Do you think every landlord would have been understanding?" Jesus asked.

"I suppose not all of them would be," Jude said. "Some people are just greedy."

"Greed?" Jesus sounded shocked. "What does greed have to do with this?"

"If they own the property—" Jude said.

"Who said they own the property?" asked Jesus.

"D-don't they?" Jude asked.

"Certainly many wealthy elites did own properties," Jesus said. "Perhaps they rented them out, but more likely they had housing for themselves for vacationing or hunting of some type. No, the *real* landlords of the day likely were paying off loans to debtors who intended to receive their money back, with a percentage. How do you think those debtors would feel to be deprived of their return in investment?"

"They all couldn't have…" Jude began.

Jesus laughed.

"I do so love you, my brother," Jesus said. "Even in despair, you hope for the best in people. But—"

A slam behind them, and all the men at the table erupted in debate. Fists were shaking, fingers pointing, spittle rocketing back and forth. Pope Gregory remained seated.

"It's simply not how humanity works," Jesus said. "Even with papal authority, the West refused to accept this initially, but purely for the reason of capitalism. Those that supported it were far more likely to be the ones receiving the money, not giving it."

"Makes sense," Jude said.

"Like those that were okay with the Nazi regime using slavery of the Jewish people for free labor," Jesus said. "And very much like what the people in your time do to people who are imprisoned for breaking the law."

"Wait," Jude stopped him. "You're telling me criminals are actually slaves?"

"The ability to work in the prison system in your country," Jesus said, "is treated as a luxury. Because it means getting out of their cells for a few hours each day. It means breaking up the monotony, or even being removed from a circumstance because corrections officers turn a blind eye when certain criminals are attacked. And they are paid pennies on the dollar of what any other business would be dismantled for paying their employees."

"So maybe it earns them time to talk to loved ones," Jude argued. "Or get some things they want otherwise."

"Your criminal justice system charges inmates an average of three dollars *per minute*. For them to speak a single minute to a loved one, that is sometimes more than a week's wages. Can you imagine having to spend months with no familial contact, not even their voice, in a place where you cannot touch other human beings? You wonder why people continue to commit crime, or, in some cases, start to commit crime when they are wrongly convicted, and expect people who are serving their time to right a wrong and still be denied their humanity."

Jude remained silent.

"That is slavery," continued Jesus. "It is treating a human as a dispensable cog in an elaborate clock with a pendulum that swings with the momentum of con artists and sycophants. They leave the system penniless, without any social supports, are expected to find a place to live, find a job, and contribute to society. Without *any* of that in place for them, prison becomes a revolving door. They go right back in and take on the same jobs, for the same low pay."

"That can't be right," said Jude.

"It is," Jesus said.

"I mean, what about the Emancipation Proclamation?" Jude asked. "Why doesn't that protect them?"

"Your country's holy Constitution," Jesus said, biting the inside of his lip. "The thirteenth amendment is the one I believe you are referring to."

"I have no clue," Jude said. "I just remember reports about slavery, Martin Luther King, Jr., and Abraham Lincoln. Emancipation Proclamation was thrown in there somewhere. Enough for me to remember it."

"Well the amendment that resulted from that specifically states that there was one exception," Jesus held up a finger for a brief moment, raising his eyebrows as it reached the climax of its trajectory. "Prisoners."

Jude scoffed, a look of disbelief on his face.

"In a system where people of color are already subjected to reminders of their status as second-class citizens in European controlled countries," Jesus said, "a system of this design was made to keep them in prison. A justice system that is objectively biased against people of color, especially if their name sounds foreign."

"How?" asked Jude. "How does that happen? Why are people like this?"

"For the most part," Jesus said, "it is not a conscious decision. A few decades before you were born, people were hung from trees by mobs purely because of the color of the person's skin. They sold postcards with pictures of these lynchings. No one was ever tried for the crimes, and when investigations *did* happen, no one would admit to being racist. And being asked if they were, or suggesting that they were, immediately shut the conversations down for them.

"They lost the point of the conversation; people were framing it around racism instead of whether a human life was lost or not. Do they do so knowingly, and with intent to be malicious?"

Jesus' face twisted into a finicky scowl.

"I would think so," said Jude. "It seems silly that someone would do something like that without knowing how it affects others."

"Like heroin users choose to become addicted," Jesus said. "Like single mothers choose to be single mothers. To have a child they're not prepared for."

"So..." Jude eased in. "You think racists are trapped in a circumstance that dictates their opinions."

"That may be part of the greater reason," Jesus replied.

Another hand slammed the table behind them, and all the voices went silent. Turning, they saw Pope Gregory standing as all the clergymen around him started to sit. He hollered at them with such rapid-fire proclamations, Jude was sure that he wouldn't understand it even if he spoke in English.

"Let me show you another one," Jesus said. "One that hits closer to home."

The Vatican bubbled away, making way for a modest, wood-paneled home. The young couple, with their child no older than a year or two, stood at attention. Before them were two Schutzstaffel officers, reading off a document. It was German, but he did recognize the very last word: "Warsaw."

A sudden clamoring from upstairs, and down came several young children and two adults. All had their arms in the air, save for the youngest who carried a stuffed bear. Two more SS officers followed behind them, guns drawn. As they proceeded out of the room, one of the officers nodded to the two interrogating the young family. After they passed, the two officers drew their weapons and fired on the mother and child. The father, in expected despair, dove for his family. Without missing a beat, the soldiers grabbed the man by the arms, dragging him from the building. The man screamed like a wild animal.

"They broke the law," Jesus said.

Jude dropped to his knees, his hand over his mouth.

"Very few people actually protected the Jewish people during this time," admitted Jesus. "There were posts throughout their cities that made the same statement: if you are out of place, or are helping to hide Jews, death is the consequence. They knew what they were getting into."

Jude's head snapped to the side to meet Jesus' gaze. "They were saving human lives," Jude shouted.

"I never said they weren't," said Jesus. "Just that they broke the law with an explicit consequence."

"Those Gentiles made the right choice," insisted Jude.

"Then not many people made the right choice," quipped Jesus. "The threat of death caused people, who would otherwise do what is right, to allow their fear to dictate their decision making."

Jude's hands clenched, and released, displaying his frustration.

"Humans are not programmed, from an evolutionary perspective, to accept death," Jesus said. "Your amygdala overpowers your rational reasoning because your brain thinks you are in danger. You cannot reason with yourself when your brain has panicked you into fighting for your life. With enough power, people's emotions can be used to regulate their behavior."

"What's your point?" demanded Jude.

"Are the people of Warsaw responsible for not taking in more Jews?" asked Jesus. "Is the blood of the Jews, those people," he gestured at the mother and child on the ground, "and others like them on the hands of the non-Jew citizens?"

Jude gritted his teeth. He cracked his knuckles as he flexed his hands.

"Were they evil?" Jesus asked in earnest. "Because they violated the law in order to save lives? In turn, ending their own?"

"It's not the same," Jude said.

"The same as what?" Jesus asked. "Not the same as telling African citizens that they are not free to leave your plantation? Not the same as telling Arab-Americans, or historically the Arabic people, how to fall in line and be American? Not the same as men who tell their wives they won't survive without them, putting them into a mental prison, believing they couldn't exist without the abusive partner?"

Jude's breath became slow and heavy.

"If not a literal prison," Jesus said, "the mental one seems to work just as well."

"So the Calendar was a good idea," Jude blurted out, anxious to change the subject. "It removed an economic harm. Then it became an immediate economic threat to average citizens."

"Correct," said Jesus.

"Because of a system that benefitted the rich," Jude continued.

"Which was already in place," Jesus said. "It forced the rare middle-class citizens to become the antagonist, driving their ire toward the wrong people."

"Then there were other systems that abused minorities," Jude went on. "Using people as property, they became prosperous off of free labor. Whether it be the south with slavery, or Nazi-occupied Europe."

"And...?" continued Jesus.

"The prison system," Jude finished.

"What is the root of all of this?" Jesus asked.

"You mean what do they have in common?" Jude replied.

"Yes."

Bringing his hands to his face, Jude rubbed his mouth as he stared upward. "Money," Jude replied.

"Yes," Jesus clapped his hands together. "This is what John's, and in turn, my ministry is about. Our people are suffering needlessly under this Empire's ever-present eye. Worse than them are the hypocrites, like the Pharisees, who enforce a tighter adherence to the Torah while asking for more tithing to the synagogue. All the while, *their* pockets are lined with money from the Romans."

Jude shook his head.

"How does James follow them?" Jude growled.

"Never mind James," said Jesus. "This is an issue bigger than James, bigger than the Pharisees. They are the gatekeepers, but they do not win." And with that, as if caught in a warp drive, the room burst into streaks of light, coming to a halt within a small room with a single bassinet. "Remember the young boy from before?" asked Jesus.

14

"No," said Jude, stepping back with his hands in the air.

"What?" asked Jesus.

"You... you can't..." stammered Jude.

"You think," said Jesus, "I'm going to ask you to kill Adolf Hitler?"

Jude peered over the side of the bassinet. This sweet, innocent child lay almost motionless on its back. His chest puffing up with each tiny breath, Jude felt sick with his instinct to swoon over the child.

"Not if you *would*," Jesus went on. "But why you wouldn't."

"I can't," said Jude. "I'm not a murderer."

"But you know that *he* is," said Jesus. "Why not stop it here? It wouldn't take much."

"No," Jude said. "No... I can't."

"Six million people," Jesus said. "Six million people die because of what this child does. You don't want to stop it before it escalates? Until it's too late?"

Jude shook his head.

"And think of the suffering you'd prevent him from," Jesus said. "You saw how mercilessly his father lashed out at him. You would be saving him from that. From having to watch his mother die."

"She'll still die," said Jude. "Then maybe she won't have anyone to be with her, to care for her. Hitler's father was an abusive monster. He would've taken his anger out on someone else. From what you say, it sounds like he did regardless. Someone else will suffer in Hitler's place."

"And what of the six million?" Jesus asked. "It sounds like the removal of Hitler from the equation changes nothing in history. Does that apply to the Holocaust?"

Jude thought for a minute.

"Well, surely Hitler wasn't alone in his thoughts," Jude reasoned.

"Tell me more," Jesus urged.

"I mean, he didn't start out shouting into microphones and having people salute him," said Jude. "He had to start—"

"Shouting in bars," Jesus said.

"So he starts by shouting his message in bars," Jude continued. "Eventually enough people want him talking for them, so they move to public forums... I mean, the guy couldn't have gained power unless there were *others* who supported him."

"And given the economic circumstances," Jesus said, "anyone could've taken the stage. Adolph just did it first."

"The Holocaust was inevitable," Jude said.

"Sadly, yes," Jesus said.

"So if I had killed Hitler?" Jude asked.

"Someone else would've taken his spot," Jesus said.

"Then it wouldn't matter," said Jude.

"There would need to be a series of significant changes to have avoided it," said Jesus.

"Was there any benefit that came from this war?" Jude asked.

"It depends who you ask," Jesus replied. "The U.S. bounced back from the Great Depression, during a time when unemployment was as high as 25%. War is a booming business. The world got the UN."

"Well, that's good I guess," said Jude.

"Would you say that was worth the life lost?" asked Jesus.

"I... don't know," admitted Jude.

"And so we come to the question of human value," said Jesus. "More importantly, the value of human life."

"Why do we even need to go there?" asked Jude. "Each life lost is one too many." Reaching his hand up to his face, Jude tried to finish the last of his wine.

"So would the ending of this one life to preserve six million in the death camps alone?" Jesus asked. "Forget the tens of millions that died fighting the war."

"But getting rid of him—" Jude began.

"Changes nothing," Jesus finished. "You know how Hitler died?"

"I've heard he was believed to have escaped to South America," Jude replied.

"Hogwash," Jesus said. "We have pieces of his skull that doctors have matched to dental records. He shot himself."

"Oh," said Jude, surrendering.

"And he did so after watching his wife die from cyanide poisoning," Jesus continued. "He had swallowed a pill himself, but was horrified at the outcome. So…" Jesus brought his hand, shaped like a gun, to his temple. His thumb slapped against his finger, mimicking the hammer slamming down on a gun.

"However it happened," Jude said, "I'm just glad he's dead."

"Is it just?" asked Jesus.

"What do you mean?" Jude asked.

"Is it just for a man," Jesus started, "who enslaved peoples of Europe, tortured them, executed them, used their personal possessions to fund his mission, people were raped, experimented on, and killed in horrific ways under his watch. Is it just that he died such a quick, and assuringly painless, death?"

"No justification would've provided closure," Jude said. "Not for the torture that came before, and I'm sure not for the memories that came after."

"So how should evil be punished?" Jesus asked.

"Well, what's evil?" asked Jude.

"Elaborate," Jesus pleaded.

"We talk about bad stuff happening," Jude said. "I don't think we disagree that there's evil in the acts you're talking about. However, with each circumstance you make me second guess the person, or situation. So… what are we talking about when we say evil?"

"It's not so much to say what is evil," said Jesus, "but is there anyone who commits evil with the *intent* of creating evil?"

"So in this situation," Jude said, "it's not just that Hitler created evil, but did he do it intentionally?"

"Yes," said Jesus.

"I would argue yes," said Jude.

"What's your reasoning?" asked Jesus.

"How could someone start a campaign against a group of people, like Hitler did?" asked Jude. "How could they start the movement with the idea that a group of people are bad, and not expect violence or murder on their behalf?"

"A little after your time," Jesus said, "there was a man who became the leader of your nation who mirrored a lot of the Nazi propaganda. He was not a brilliant man, but he knew the distaste and fears of the people he wanted to win over." Waving his hand, the nursery gave way to a large gymnasium. One that looked like a modern coliseum.

Though not filled, the gym contained a large group of people, maybe a few hundred, and a stage with a podium. As with the scenario with Hitler, there was an older man yelling to the group, but this man had orange-looking skin, a red tie too long for his body, and strange-looking blondish-gray hair. His arms waved, often mirroring one another, as if he held an invisible accordion in his hand. At various points, the audience cheered, booed softly, or would shout random phrasing at the speaker.

"He is merciless in his hatred," said Jesus. "He cares not for women, for those affected by poverty, the sick, or anyone whose skin is not white."

"In America?" asked Jude. "There's no way this guy—"

"That's exactly what the rest of the people who think like you thought," Jesus interrupted. "And yet…" Jesus pointed in the direction of the man behind the podium.

"He targets Mexicans," Jesus said. "He gives them labels with no justification. People who look like me? They become targets because he tells people they are terrorists. He says we are part of a religious fundamentalist group that views the slaughter of innocent lives as justice for their suffering. And Jews?" Jesus shook his head.

"I can't understand…" Jude started. "How…?"

"People fear what they do not understand," said Jesus. "This man claimed that white citizens were in distress and being ignored, because people were made aware of how people of color are treated in your country. How women are treated. On the surface, this man espoused ideas that connected him to the average people that lived in your country. Behind the scenes, he threw away regulations that protected the planet, the people, their income, and their ability to work. Did he know what he was doing? Yes. And he viewed it all as repayment for what he felt was his being wronged.

"Hitler was the same in Germany," Jesus continued. "He built himself off of the fears of others, not everyone agreed with—or liked—him, but he rode that momentum all the way into a position of power. A position others helped him get into, and one that allowed him to take control of the people in a way that benefitted him and his colleagues. Perhaps his nationalism drove him, but his justification, good or bad, led him to do inhuman things to other people."

"Are you telling me all this to get me to turn you over to the Romans?" Jude asked.

Jesus looked up at Jude. "Yes," he replied. "Because I know you're a good man being asked to do a terrible thing."

Rubbing his hands on his face, Jude sighed.

"I know it's a lot," Jesus said, "but if you don't, the outcome is another parallel universe that, not only doesn't acknowledge my existence,

128

but ultimately leads up to a possible future where you are no longer living."

"No," Jude shook his head.

"Your family," Jesus said. "Your mother and father, they were forced from their homes as children due to micro aggressions and outright assaults from Christian members of their respective communities. If the belief had not been in place, one where the Jews are demonized by Christians, they would not have met. Moving further back, thanks to Hitler's strict belief that Jews were a mongrel race and close collusion with the Vatican, the Holocaust is altered, and your grandparents never flee Germany."

Jude froze, his muscles twitching.

"Those few things," Jesus continued, "while seemingly minute, are later changes that inevitably end in your non-existence."

"So I—" Jude started.

"Never go back in time," Jesus said. "Because you're never born. Whether that creates a whole new multiverse, or a single universe, you will eventually be erased from time. By your *not* contributing to my timeline, you are eventually erased."

"Be remembered as the traitor of the Messiah," Jude said. "Or disappear."

"Jude," Jesus said. "You're a tortured man. You've experienced so much in such a short time. Whether you're remembered as the one fulfilling your role to bring about the Christian movement, or you become lost to time as another person becomes the leader of the next religious movement, is on the individual receiving the story. Yet the one who is being put to death *knows* why it is being done, why you are doing it. And the Son of Man will forgive you."

15

Jude's hands shook as he looked at them; they quivered as if he were stranded in the cold. His mind raced, and he felt as if the atmospheric pressure had compressed around his body. The muscles in his body all felt as though they were tensing for an impact he was unaware was about to occur.

Jude walked the pathway leading up to the gateway of Jerusalem. His brothers, Judith, Rachel, and his mother, all walked in a collective group. Jesus escorted a foal, with supplies and food for their stay. Simon stood next to Jesus, carrying a sack with items for their excursion to the Temple for Passover. James was somewhere in the crowd, but where they couldn't say. James had made his way out to the Temple with the Pharisees, as he had done for the last several years. Otherwise, they were joined by the other followers of Jesus. Men, women, their families, all followed close to Jesus and his family as they trekked in.

A soft, gentle hand reached out and held Jude's left hand. "It's going to be alright," Judith said.

"I don't know if I can do this," Jude whispered to her.

"Yes, you can," Judith assured him.

They moved at a cautious pace along the stone pathway. Jude was covered in sweat, his arms twitching as if he were being electrocuted at a spontaneous rate while wiping away his sweat. In spite of the tension across his body, his muscles quaking with each movement, his knees felt like gelatin. Each step felt like trying to hold up the world. And in his head, he knew that was true.

"I want a drink," Jude lamented.

"Are you sure?" Judith asked.

"W-water," Jude stammered. He looked up at her with mournful eyes.

"Of course," she jumped.

Pulling out a wine skin, and taking a swig from it first, Judith handed the bottle to Jude. "That's water," she said.

Jude gulped in a feverish demonstration, squeezing and twisting the skin to remove the last few drops.

"Better?" she asked.

Jude retched onto the ground.

"Jude?" called Jesus from the front. He handed the reigns of the foal to Thomas, rushing back to assist. Jesus put his arms around Jude, helping him to keep walking.

"You need wine," Jesus said.

"No," Jude shook his head. His trembling hand rose up to wipe away the vomit that stuck to his beard.

"My brother," he pleaded. "You know this is how things are supposed to be. Abstaining from—"

"I can't..." Jude explained. "I just can't."

"Jude," Jesus shook him with a soft push from his hands. "You know what happens if you choose not to."

"Well," said Jude, stopping to gag. Spitting, he continued. "Maybe it's best I do it with a clear uninhibited mind."

Jude tapped the side of his head, winking at Jesus.

"Judas," pleaded Judith. "Listen to him."

"No," said Jude. "I'm fine."

"Judas, my brother," Jesus stopped, turning to stand before Jude, his arms crossed. The crowd around Jesus halted with him. "You are so important for what must happen," Jesus said. "I implore you, please just have a drink. Just one, so you are not suffering during our journey in."

Jude shook his head. "Just let me walk," he said.

Jesus scowled. "Then at least let me walk with you," he said. Nodding at Judith, they each put one of Jude's arms over their respective shoulders. Hoisting him up, they steadied Jude as he shook with each step.

Levi stepped up alongside them. Peering through the corner of his eye, he uncorked his wine skin and started to sip from the container. At one point, a light drizzle of red fell from his mouth, through his beard. Jude shot daggers at him from his eyes. Had he the strength, Jude thought of the satisfaction of allowing his knuckles to connect with Levi's jaw. Instead, he blew a kiss at Levi.

"Canaanite," Levi called at him.

"Ph-Pharisee!" Jude responded.

Levi pivoted and started toward Jesus and Jude. Judith jumped in between Levi and Jude. Jesus' hand went up, his eyes ablaze. Levi frowned at Jesus and Jude, stepping back toward the group of people he had been with before.

"A true gift from God," Judith said with a cynical tone.

"Jesus!" called Simon from the front.

Looking forward, Jesus saw Simon and Thomas pointing ahead. The gate entrance was only a few meters before them. It was littered with Roman guards, staring down over the large groups of people entering the city. Waves of voices, hollering, laughing, crying, and shouting sales over, and through, one another was overflowing from the walls.

"Judith," Jesus said.

"Go on," she said, nodding at him.

Jesus leapt forward, weaving his way through others like a snake through grass. Reaching the foal, Jesus bounced up, throwing his leg over the animal. He gripped straps tied down over the foal's back, smiling down at Simon and Thomas. The former held his hand over his mouth, stifling a laugh. As they passed through the entryway, Simon whipped a palm branch out from his robes. Running forward, pushing people out of the way, Simon laid down the branch in front of Jesus and the foal.

"All hail the Son of Man," Simon hollered, bowing to Jesus.

Thomas ran out, placing another palm branch after Simon's.

"All hail!" Thomas announced, turning to face the crowd. Many with their eyes turned, darting between him and the guards above.

"That's enough," called down one of the centurions, waving his hand to dismiss the trouble makers.

"*All hail the Son of Man!*" called a woman's voice. Jude looked up to see his mother, Mary, placing a palm branch before Jesus.

"All hail!" others called.

In a swarm, a large percentage of the crowd started to surge toward them. Many held palm branches in their hands.

"Enough of this mockery!" shouted down another centurion.

Many of the guards had turned and were staring down at the Jews with fury.

"Behold!" cried a passerby.

A woman ran over and laid a palm branch, bowing and laughing up toward the guards.

"All hail!" cried a man, running over to place a palm branch as he waved up at the Romans.

Others started to cry out similar phrases, the distinct sound of palm branches being pulled from hiding, broken from some of the nearby trees. In droves, people rushed in front of Jesus to place branches tracing a path through the entrance. Shouts and growls from the upper tier of the gate was drowned out by the calls from the Jews.

"Behold our king!" some shouted.

"Long live the Twelve Tribes!" called others.

It was clear the Romans took no pleasure in watching the display. Some whispered to themselves, pointing down at Jesus. Others shouted warnings at the citizens, slamming their spears against the flooring below them. Some, with swords drawn, waved them at the people, or pointed toward Jesus as they hurled insults.

Jude, smiling as he watched the display, looked toward Jesus. A welcome distraction from his maladies. Jesus had a noble look as he sat upon the foal. His body still as a statue, Jesus gave no recognition to the Romans or the people around him. Pulling away from Judith, Jude lurched forward, pressing his way up to Jesus.

"Judas, wait," called Judith.

He paid her no mind, reaching out between the few people before him. Reaching the foal, Jude stretched out and grasped one of the restraints. Holding on and pulling himself up to Jesus, Jude looked up to see what he was doing. With eyes closed, Jesus swayed from side to side. His face stone-like, the corners of his mouth twitching with tension in his face. Tears were streaked down his cheeks. As if in a meditative state, Jesus' hands held together like a bear trap. His thumbs circled one another with an anxious fidget.

"Jesus," Jude called up. His hand spasming like charges of electricity rocketed through his nerves. "I'm with you, my brother."

Jesus' hand, freed, moved toward Jude in a smooth, graceful gesture. His hand stopping mere inches from his face, Jude reached up and held his hand.

"My brother," Jesus said. "I feel your agony."

"And I yours," Jude consoled him.

"Just do what your body tells you to do," Jesus said.

"I can't..." Jude started, his convulsions taking over his behavior. "I can't... d-d-do what you need of me."

"But I need you to," said Jesus, squeezing Jude's hand. "I need you."

Looking behind them, Jude swore he saw the guards looking, and pointing, at him. His gaze moved ahead, focusing on the wall between them and the inner courtyard. Inside were merchants some selling animals for the sacrifice and items to make their bread, and others money changers. Centurions along the top stared down at Jude and Jesus. All but confirming Jude's theory they were paying attention to him, he made eye contact with one centurion who turned to another looking at him as well. Whispering to him, the man being spoken to nodded, pivoted, and walked out of sight.

Jude's mind became awash with an elaborate scheme: the Romans were going to come after Jesus' family. This was further exacerbated by looking at how Jesus held his hand. *I'm the closest to Jesus. They'll come for me first*, Jude thought. Heart pounding against his chest, Jude's spasming became worse. It was like being on the cusp of vomiting; it's coming, and it's coming now.

Jude looked frantically around for an exit, his hand pulling away from Jesus. Two hands grabbed Jude and directed him forward.

"*It's okay*," came the warm, comforting voice behind him.

"J-J-J..." Jude stammered. He grimaced as he fought to work out the words. "J-Judith?" he finally asked.

"I'm here," she said, rubbing his lower back.

It was instant bliss. Her voice, guiding him from panic to placid, reminded him of all the gentle goodnights she offered. Her telling of stories as the family prepared for bed. Her gentleness, her compassion, always grounded Jude. Her touch, like so many before, was always shocking and soothing all at once. Jude had always felt the most loved when he was touched, and hers felt like the first kiss of every new skin of wine.

"Why do you do this to yourself?" she asked.

"I-I can't," Jude conceded. "Can't drink if sobriety m-means I save our brother.

"This is what is to happen," she said. "You cannot shirk your responsibilities to the greater good."

Jude didn't answer.

"This means you won't exist," Judith said.

Jude snapped his head toward Judith.

"How do you know this?" Jude demanded. "Jesus didn't reveal it to anyone else."

"But I know my brother's fate," she said. "This is what's to happen to help bring the kingdom of God to Earth. The New Jerusalem."

"Ju-Judith," Jude pleaded. "You know what is r-r-relevant for… for history."

"You talk in your sleep," Judith stopped him.

"I… what?" Jude said, dumbfounded.

"If you don't do what's asked of you," she said, "I know your parents will never meet. So you won't be born."

Jude was silent.

"Jude," she asked. "I know something bad will happen once Jesus has died. I will treasure what little time I have left with him, but I am scared things will not go well if you do not perform your purpose." She gripped Jude's face by his chin, turning his face toward her. "And I am worried for you," she said, tears welling up in her eyes.

As they passed through the entryway into the courtyard, Jesus dismounted his foal. Thomas took her by the reigns and guided her away, along the outer edges of the courtyard. Looking over to Simon, Bartholomew, and several of the other apostles, Jesus nodded, and they scattered out to various stations.

"W-what are they doing?" Jude asked.

Judith smiled and said, "Starting the revolution."

Turning his attention back to Jesus, Jude watched him approach one of the money changers' tables. He bounced up and down as he looked around himself. Simon, Bartholomew, and several others were standing at other stations, watching Jesus.

Looking upward, Jesus observed the centurions having gone back to their stations. Their attention turned down to the activity before them in the entrance. Others argued with other Jews, some opting to kick stones down onto them. Several glanced with passing interest over Jesus.

Jude saw several staring at him. His attention wrenched back around as he heard a loud *bang*, clattering of coins, and shouting voices.

"You turn our Father's house into a den of thieves!" Jesus shouted.

Across the vast courtyard, similar bangs continued, coins scattering and pinging off of rocks and each other on the ground. Shouting erupted from several areas, turning the arena into a swirl of echoes, loud jarring crashes, and screams as several money turners grabbed the apostles and assaulted them.

Jude's chest tightened, crouching down as he found it harder to breathe.

"My love," cried Judith, crouching beside him.

Centurions turned and stared down at the anarchy that had erupted. They hollered down at the crowds, several guards pointing at Jesus, and Jude, again. Several disappeared, only to burst through the crowd toward the apostles and Jesus.

"F-F-Fuck," gurgled Jude through gritted teeth.

"Relax," Judith consoled him. "And behold."

She pointed at the center of the courtyard, and Jude looked up with bewilderment in his eyes. The crowd encircled the men, joining and locking arms as they closed in around them.

"You desecrate our Father's house!" Jesus hollered. "Your merchants trade money to people who have no concept of math! They steal from those with nothing!" Jesus spun around, gesturing at a group of robed men. With dark maroon colors, and a gold sash with matching cuffs, a collection of rabbis descended upon the scene. "And look who we have?" cheered Jesus, clapping his hands over his face. "My dear brother, the hypocrite."

Out of the group emerged James; his beard speckled with grey hairs. His headdress, matching the others', looked almost Egyptian.

Jesus smirked. "Indeed, it seems you're now serving our former slave owners," he chuckled.

"Watch your tongue, you welp," James quipped. "It will be a grand day when our Father brings judgement upon the world. I will personally reserve front row seats to see you cast into Gehenna!"

"Brother," Jesus hollered back, pulling Mary to his side. "You are always welcome to join your family again."

"Do not tempt me, *shatan*!" James hollered, throwing an accusing finger at him.

"Betrayer!" Simon shouted, thrusting forward and being caught by Mary. Pulling him close to her, she caressed his hair and whispered something in his ear with her eyes closed. Simon's chest heaved as he glared at James. Jesus placed a hand on Simon's shoulder.

"You would be proud of your baby brother," Jesus called to James. "He truly has become the rock that others will build their faith from."

James glared at them, his finger still pointed, arm relaxed. He chewed the inside of his lower lip, like something was dying to escape his mouth.

"Your pockets are lined with blood money," Jesus called. "Thou shall have no graven images."

The men behind James hollered in protest, demanding capture of the instigators.

"They are an affront to our Lord!" one screamed.

"They twist Yahweh's word!" another yelped.

"He is cursed!" others hollered in unison.

One broke through the group, shoving James aside. He thrust to the ground a woman in tattered clothing, her breasts exposed, bruises on her arms and face. Dried blood traced from her right nostril down to her collar bone. Sand was caked onto the blood, with dirt and grime smeared all over her body.

"What say you?" screamed the Pharisee, pointing at the woman.

"Monster," Jude growled, lunging forward. Judith tightened her grip around him.

"Be still," she whispered. "Save your energy."

"What is it you're asking?" Jesus responded.

"She is an adulteress," the Pharisees responded. The others behind him yelled taunts and jeers at the group. The crowd closed in a tight barrier around the woman. She lay on the ground, her arms up over her head. She trembled in the same way Jude was.

"I deserve worse," Jude groaned.

"What?" Judith asked.

"Look what they did to her…" he lamented. "I feel that. But I never went through what she did."

"Stop that," she insisted. "This is not about you."

Jude paused.

"What is your name?" Jesus called to the woman.

"Why do you care?" called the Pharisee, the others shouting in kind.

"Mary," came a choked, airy reply.

Jesus glanced down at the woman. She looked up at him, her face twisted in agony and fear.

"Mary," Jesus responded, kneeling down. "That's my mother's name," he continued, pointing to his mother.

"Magdalene," she continued.

"Yeshua ben Yosef," Jesus said. "They're saying some pretty serious stuff about you." The woman sniffed, her lip trembling. "I don't know what happened," said Jesus. "I wasn't there. Could you tell me what happened?"

Her mouth opened a few times, only to release exasperated gasps.

"It was the morning after her wedding," called James.

All eyes turned toward him. He had shape shifted into a statuesque storyteller, thrusting his chest forward as he spoke.

"Her husband stood outside," James continued, "awaiting the passing of the Pharisees to our morning prayers. He had produced the sheets of their bed where they consummated the marriage and there was no blood."

139

Jesus looked to Mary. Her eyes looking up from the ground with terror. "Is this true?" he asked her.

She nodded, covering her eyes as tears dripped from her chin.

"My brother," Jesus asked as he stood. "What does this prove?"

"She was not a virgin on her wedding night," James replied. "Her hymen was not intact."

"And was she pregnant?" asked Jesus.

James shook his head. "What?" he cried.

"Was she pregnant prior to last evening?" Jesus clarified.

"Why does that matter?" James called.

"These are laws in issues of paternity," Jesus called. "Was she pregnant before last night?"

"I…" James hesitated.

"It does not matter," called the Pharisee who had thrown the woman to the ground. "You would side with an adulteress, being a bastard!"

Simon started to unsheathe a small blade, his hand caressing it like an ancient urn.

"My parents were married when my brothers and I were born," Jesus snapped. "But I know you were the result of a high priest having an affair with a poor handmaid."

The Pharisee's mouth dropped. The others began to clamor behind him.

"How else do you think you received the education you did?" asked Jesus. "How did you get into such an elite position? I bet it has to do with the payoff of benefits like the ones our patriarchs reaped the rewards from; things like treating women as objects, possessions."

"How dare you?" he screamed.

"Your mother was a paid for house cleaner," Jesus continued. "And when she became pregnant, the full-time nanny. Wet nurse. Sex object. And you know you have full-blooded siblings, don't you?"

"You shut your accursed mouth!" the Pharisee shrieked.

"They're all either slaves to other land owners," Jesus called, "or handmaids themselves. And you never did a thing to stop it."

"Crucify him!" the Pharisee screamed at the guards.

Swords in sheaths, the guards glanced around at the large number of Jews standing at the ready to fight. Several turned and looked at commanding officers, all who were judging the situation. One by one, as they started shaking their heads, the guards turned and left the courtyard. The Pharisees, seeing their protection walk away, panicked and started running through any open doorway.

The crowd pulled their arms out from between each other. Glancing around, they smiled at one another; they were beaming as they realized what they had done. Some started to clap, silenced by others.

"Don't push your luck," someone said as they grabbed a person attempting to clap.

James stood by as the people began to disperse around the courtyard. His eyes fixed on Jesus, he turned as if moving through sludge. He walked back through the entryway opposite Jesus and his disciples.

Judith squeezed Jude close. "Can you believe that?" she whispered. "Look what our brother did." Bringing him over to an empty seat beside an overturned table, Judith stroked Jude's back. "I have to go help Mother for a moment," she said. Jude looked over her shoulder and saw Mary holding a knife in her hand, shaking her head.

Simon's head hung low as Jesus stood over him, lecturing with an authoritative look.

"I'll be fine," Jude grumbled. His body shook as he was overcome with an arctic chill.

"Are you sure?" Judith asked, raising an eyebrow at Jude.

"I'm fine," Jude said, waving her away. "Nothing a quick rest won't fix."

Judith smirked in uncertainty, looking back and forth between Jude and her mother. Her decision to help with the knife situation taking precedence over Jude's pride, she dashed away.

Alone for less than a moment, several hands grabbed ahold of Jude and covered his mouth. The pressure from his assailant's hands was so forceful, Jude was unable to swivel his head and see a face.

But those hats.

16

Thrown to the ground, Jude rolled onto his side and pulled himself into the fetal position. He felt his ribs crack as he landed. A short, wet scream gurgled into grunts, enunciated with sopping gasps.

"My poor brother," came a familiar, cynical voice. "How far down the sinner's hole have we gone? After all, God does not punish the just. God punishes the wicked."

Jude chuckled, sputtering into coughs as his face contorted between amused and anguished. Blood trickled out the corner of his mouth.

"Is that… is that w-why you're James the J-Just?" Jude choked out, hacking and laughing in response.

"You mock me," James replied, gliding over to Jude. "But we'll see what happens to your little movement by tomorrow."

"You don't…" Jude coughed. "You don't have the n-numbers. His body trembled as he fought to catch his breath.

No response came at first. They all seemed to sit and relish Jude grunting and shaking, the hacking up of blood.

"You're right," James admitted at last. "But we have our ways."

A wine skin slapped on the ground beside Jude. Uncapped, the wine splashed against his face. Jude closed his eyes, finding himself recalling the comfort of being in his mother's lap. His father's embrace, with the aroma of the wine on his breath. The smell of the sifter his mother used to drink out of. Tears dripped over the bridge of his nose.

"You will have your fill of wine," James called to him. "Provided you bring us to where your location is tonight."

Jude choked out a sob.

"This isn't about you," James said. "This is about respecting the laws of those who help protect us. The Romans permit us to worship freely, so long as Herod has no trouble makers. First there was John, and now…" Jude reached out and dragged the wine skin to his lips, suckling at the open mouth of the container as the wine drizzled out. "We'll expect to see you after the Seder," James finished. Turning to the others, James nodded and they filed out from the alleyway they were in.

Jude lifted the wine skin, swallowing with a fury as each drop hit his lips. Each gulp was accented with a sharp sting in his side, the pain causing him to sneer and lose half of the contents in his mouth each time. Dropping the wine skin, he sobbed in a hushed choke. "My God, My God," Jude cried to himself. "Why have you forsaken me?"

Something Jude hadn't seen in what felt like an eternity manifested before him with a glowing doorway with a lone figure exiting from it. Tears blurred his vision, his pain distracted him and made it difficult to focus. The figure approached him with a slow saunter. As the tears dribbled down his face, he saw a slender, toned man with olive skin and finely braided hair. His long beard, flecked with white hair that made him look similar to James, covered all but the depraved smile painted across the man's face.

"*Hey Juuuuuude*," the man sang, mimicking the Liverpudlian accent of the Beatles. "*Don't be afraid…*" he continued, kneeling down just in front of Jude's face.

"A little confused, are we?" he asked. Jude coughed out a wad of blood and mucus. "Well, I guess I owe you an explanation," the man said. "After all, I'm the one responsible for bringing you here."

An orb, like Jesus had produced before, grew just behind the man. Within the orb, Jude witnessed the scene with the young boy who forced him here. The crazy eyes, the twisted smile. As Jude watched himself fall through the open portal in the scene, the orb dissipated into the ether.

"Yeah," said the man. "You give a kid a power like what my son and I share, and there are some specific casualties along the way."

Jude wheezed in response.

"See kid," the man explained, "there's this other thing I should explain too. Your parents went through some tough shit in front of you. Some of that was your father accusing your mother of infidelity. And there's a reason for that."

Jude's eyes gazed up toward the man.

"See, your mother happens to have had a one-night stand with another fellow right around the time you were conceived," the man said. "So your father, not knowing if he was your dad or not, decided to take a chance and assume you were his."

Jude's lip shook.

"I'm sad to tell you," the man continued, "he was not your father."

Jude scowled as he tried to stop the sobs. His face contorting into more painful shapes as lightning shot up and down his side.

"Don't confuse that for not loving you," he continued. "That was his struggle; how could someone who was not biologically your father love you so deeply."

Jude struggled to control his spasming, wet groans spurting out like Morse code.

"He didn't care," said the man. "For your sake, your relationship, he didn't care. But for your mother's lack of gratitude for his forgiveness, for his sacrifice and devotion to your family. She gave him a child that was unquestionably his, genetic testing and all. But that was something he never required of you."

Jude wiped tears from his face, with slow, intentional movements.

"Your mother felt trapped," he said. "Indebted to a man who still took her in, despite her infidelity. But he never forgave her. The accusations, while never calling back to her original sin indefinitely, sure did center around behavior she exhibited prior to being caught."

Jude continued to wheeze, reaching inside his tunic.

145

"So she never…" he hesitated. "Well, did you ever put together that your birthdate is only two weeks after their wedding?"

Jude's brow furrowed as his hand sunk deeper into his clothing.

"Yeah," the man concluded. "You're a modern-day Solomon alright."

Jude grunted, his forearm half submerged in his tunic.

"And, just to confirm," the man continued. "Jesus *is* your brother. And, hello! I'm your daddy!"

Holding out his arm, Jude hollered as he grasped the man's wrist, whipping out a knife and slashing it across the man's arm. Blood ripped from the wound, spreading in an arch over him. But the righteous satisfaction Jude felt was torn from him as the man and the blood appeared to evaporate in front of him. With a blink, Jude found himself locked in a tight embrace. One arm was around his throat, Jude noticed a long scar dragging up the inside of the man's forearm. The other arm was holding Jude's wrist that gripped the knife.

"You've got a fight in you," the familiar voice said. His breath stank of hard liquor, the kind Jude's grandfather used to drink. "That's how I know you're my kid. You were born to incite change, to spark an uprising."

Jude gurgled out a shout in protest. The man squeezed tighter, choking off part of Jude's airway.

"Your people," the man said. "Our people, the people of this promised land, are subjugated under an imperialist rule. They pay taxes so the 'protectors' can put graven images in their Temple, one they will destroy when the people rise up."

Jude tugged at the arm around his neck, gasping in distress through what tiny air space he had.

"This is not about you," he said. "Just do what you are destined to do."

146

With as much warning as he had given when he appeared, the mysterious man was gone. Jude collapsed, dropping the knife, gagging for air.

"Jude!" came a concerned call, followed by rapid footsteps.

"Oh, my brother," came the voice of Jesus.

"Is he okay?" cried Simon.

"Hold on," Jesus called.

Jude felt a warm vibration as his ribs shifted. Sharp, stabbing pain rocketed up through his side. The suddenness, and severity, of the pain caused Jude to tense up, twisting as each bone popped back into place. His lungs, clearing to a rattle, dwindled in slow developments. At last, his breathing turned to a normal sound, paced in good comfort.

"Jesus?" came a soft call from Jude.

"My dear brother," Jesus said, turning him on his back.

Jude relaxed as he looked up at Jesus.

"Brother," Jude whispered, a smile oozed out of the corners of his mouth.

"I'm so glad you're okay," Jesus said, standing up.

Jude held out his hands, Jesus and Simon each taking one as they lifted Jude to his feet. Simon, glancing down at the wine skin on the ground, pointed and looked up at Jude. "What say you?" he asked.

Jude looked at Jesus, his eyebrows creased into a tent shape. Leave it to his baby brother to allow for his naiveté to ask what everyone was wondering. Looking back at the wine skin, Jude walked over and scooped it up. Bringing the opening to his lips, he guzzled down the remnants of the sour stinging wine. With his last gulp, Jude threw aside the skin and rubbed the tears from his eyes. Looking back and forth between the men, Jude sighed.

Clearing his throat, Jude broke the silence and said, "As it is foretold in the scriptures."

17

Jesus poured wine into his cup, taking care to not pour more than half a glass. He passed it on to Simon, who was huddled up against Jesus. Other apostles looked at Simon with disdain; how could this bootlicking urchin do this in front of everyone?

"If he's not careful," Bartholomew grumbled, "someone's going to start calling him Jesus' 'beloved.'"

Sniggers seeped out of some of the apostles' mouths. Levi slipped a loud "ha!" before slapping his hand over his mouth.

"HA!" Jude hollered back across the table, slamming his hands down as he leapt to his feet. All eyes focused on Jude, who stared down the table toward Bartholomew and Levi. "Watch your tongue," Jude slurred. "Or I'll make sure that *you're* the beloved!"

The men seated among Bartholomew and Levi shifted uncomfortably in their seats, examining their glasses.

"Cowards," Jude grumbled as he dropped back into his seat.

The others among them were passing along large, torn pieces of unleavened bread. As it passed to each hand, another chunk was torn and placed before someone. Several jars of wine sat around the table. Jude had secured one in front of himself. The others knew enough to allow Jude to drink whenever he wanted. He was, after all, Jesus' closest brother.

Judith, seated beside Jude, looked at him with concern. "My dear," she begged. "Can you slow down?" Jude looked down into his glass, swirling it in a counter-clockwise motion. "I just don't want you getting aggressive," she admitted. "I know how you get with tension and conflict."

"Do you?" Jude snapped.

Judith paused, bringing her hands to his back and rubbing in small circles. "I just don't want you to get in trouble," she sighed. Jesus was eyeing them as he tore off a small piece of his bread. Judith smirked in discomfort back at Jesus, rubbing Jude's back. "Please," she pleaded. "For me?"

Still spinning his glass, Jude sneered and nodded his head. "I'm sorry," he said. "I don't mean to——"

"I know," she said. "I understand why you feel so anxious."

Judith's arms came around Jude and she hugged him tight. Jude closed his eyes and basked in her warmth, like the first day of spring when the snow melted. He felt the warm breeze, heard the sound of their rain boots running through the soaked yards, browned from a season with no sunlight and frozen turf. He remembered his mother sitting on the front steps of their home, cheering him on as he performed menial tasks like they were Olympic events. Jude smiled, and kissed Judith's arm.

Everyone's head turned as Jesus pushed back his chair and stood before the few dozen that sat around the small enclosure. Raising his glass, he cleared his throat.

"Brothers and sisters," Jesus pronounced. "I am truly blessed, truly grateful, for your presence with us this evening. Some of you have been present since the beginning of John's ministry, and finding relevance in mine, followed me. I am honored to be your representative."

The others raised their glasses; calls of "*hear, hear,*" and "*blessed is the coming kingdom,*" rose from the group. They all drank in turn.

"You should know," Jesus cried out, demanding attention, "I will not always be here with you."

Gasps and hollers rang out among his followers. Seats shifted and several stood.

Simon's head drooped as he wiped away tears.

"You can already see it in the faces of the guards," Jesus continued. "As outnumbered as they were, it will not always be that way. They will apprehend me." Lifting his glass, he said to them, "I will not again drink the fruit of the vine until the Kingdom of God comes for me." He drank from his cup, the others following suit.

"*My Lord,*" called a voice from the other end of the table.

"Andrew?" Jesus asked.

Andrew, a rugged looking man, stood and clutched his meaty, calloused hands together. His fingers gyrated between one another like wriggling maggots.

"Lord," Andrew continued. "You are so wise, and you've predicted coming events so accurately. Could… could you tell us…?"

Andrew swallowed as his eyes scanned with caution around the room.

"Could I tell you, what?" asked Jesus.

"Well," Andrew blurted out. "How do they find you? We are here in secret, are we not?"

Jesus nodded.

"So," Andrew's eyes looked for answers, "that would mean someone would need to… to betray us?"

Jesus stared ahead at Andrew, an eyebrow rising.

"Does that seem plausible?" Jesus asked.

Andrew looked over the faces in the room.

"Who told?!" Andrew hollered. The others leaned away, holding their hands up as if his accusation might pierce them.

"Andrew!" Jesus snapped.

"I'll have you hog-tied!" Andrew yelled. "I won't allow our Savior, our Messiah, to—"

"Andrew!" Jesus hollered, causing Andrew to stumble back into his seat. "If you do not lower your voice, everyone will have you to thank for alerting the Romans to our location."

Andrew sat up in his seat, rubbing at his eyes. He nodded with excitement, clutching the sides of his seat with white knuckles.

"Apologize," Simon snarled, standing at attention.

Everyone glanced toward Simon, connecting his gaze back toward Andrew.

"Simon," Jesus pleaded.

"You do not get to question my brother's plan," Simon shot through gritted teeth.

"Simon, no," Jesus' tone took a sharp authoritative turn. Simon took deep intentional breaths through flared nostrils. "Relax," Jesus begged.

"Don't act all high and mighty," Jude shouted at Simon.

Simon and Jesus both looked toward Jude, who was pouring another glass of wine. He emptied the pitcher into his glass, slamming it down on the table.

"You're not going to be able to ride that high horse for too much longer," Jude said, bringing his glass to his lips.

Simon's eyes filled with tears. "Never," he susurrated. "Never." His hand gripped the sleeves of Jesus' tunic, pulling him closer. Jesus wrapped his arms around Simon, allowing him to sob into his neck.

"Be strong, my rock," Jesus said. "I need your strength."

The others nibbled at their bread, sipped their wine, and murmured among themselves.

"*He looks possessed...*" Jude heard one say.

"*...shatan...*" came another claim.

Jude knocked back the last of his wine, stuffing what remained of his bread into this mouth.

"Jude," Jesus called over with the reservation of someone telling a friend their mother was going to die. Jude looked up, chewing like a cow against the wad of bread in his mouth. Jesus looked back, consoling Simon in his arms. His eyes locking with Jude's. "Quickly," Jesus said. "Go do what it is you need to do."

Jude wept, dropping his face into his hands. Stifling the cries, he snorted and choked as he rose from his chair. Judith rose behind him, rubbing his back as he stood.

"No, Judith," Jesus pleaded. "Stay."

Bringing her hands up to her face, Judith sat as she looked with sorrow upon Jude. His eyes red and puffy, Jude rubbed the moisture from his cheeks and exited the house.

18

"Brother!" James called out.

Jude marched with hesitation toward the high priests, seated in a semi-circle around a small podium. James walked out to greet Jude, guiding him toward the stand. "Please," he said, gesturing to the podium.

Jude stumbled as he paced forward, an opened, and full, wine skin in his hands. Reaching the podium, Jude took a swig from the skin. Gasping as he swallowed, Jude used his sleeve to wipe away at his beard.

"Have you..." James started. "Have you considered what we asked of you earlier?"

Jude nodded, swaying as he stood.

"What say you?" hollered one of the priests. "Where is the so-called 'Messiah?'"

The Pharisees chortled with laughter. Others groaned lamenting the title used.

"I want..." Jude held up a finger. "I want one thing first."

Chuckles swirled through the walls of the temporary tabernacle they had constructed. It looked like a traveling tent for royalty.

"What is it?" asked James.

"Don't tchhhh..." Jude slurred. Stopping himself, licking his lips, he carried on. "Don't *touch* anyone else."

"Oh," called out one of the priests. "You need not worry. *We* won't touch anyone."

"Romans however…" cried another voice, the men bursting into laughter.

"No," hollered Jude. "You tell them, no one else should b-be… hurt. Or captured."

Jude's knees gave out, catching himself by the edges of the podium. He pulled himself back up into a standing position. The priests laughed at him.

"Jude," spoke James. "You know we cannot promise anyone else's safety. That is dependent on how they respond to the centurions. If they provoke them, then…" James shrugged. "And let's not forget," he continued, "unless you cooperate, you are guilty of conspiracy to instigate an insurrection against the Roman Empire. That carries with it a penalty of crucifixion."

Jude gulped as his hands shook, his vision in and out of focus.

"And," James said, "there is always an opportunity for you here, with us." He gestured toward an empty chair. One that was located next to where James had been sitting.

Jude choked back the sobs that tried to escape.

"What do you say?" James asked, bringing the wine skin Jude had dropped up to his lips. As he did, the wine cascaded down into his mouth. The fruity, acidic sting as it slid down the back of his throat. His shoulders relaxed. The tension in his neck disappeared. His knees bent. As James pulled back with the wine skin, Jude smacked his lips, swallowing the wine in a single gulp. "And now?" James asked.

Jude paused; his eyes closed as he savored the fresh tastes in his mouth. "Gethsemane," he muttered.

"I'm sorry?" asked James.

"Gethsemane," Jude repeated, bringing the wine skin back to his lips.

James turned and looked at the rest of the priests. Smug smiles and sandpaper giggling sounded off between several members. James turned back, a smile painted on his face. He approached Jude, placing a hand on his shoulder. James pulled Jude in for a hug, patting his hand on his back like he was putting out a fire with his palms.

"Thank you, brother," James whispered. Pulling away, his hands resting on Jude's shoulders, James sighed. "I know you've been through a lot, brother," James said. "But I need you to do one final thing for me."

After sipping another quick gulp from the skin, Jude held out his hand before James. Smiling, James went into a cabinet and withdrew a fresh wine skin. Placing it in Jude's open palm, he uncorked it and brought it to his lips. With a sigh, Jude scratched the top of his head. He licked at the small patch of flesh just under his septum that never grew hair.

"You need me to identify him," Jude said.

19

Jude stumbled up the path as he and the Roman centurions marched toward the smoke they saw in the distance. It was expected that, though Jesus and the apostles were in hiding, they didn't think anyone would notice them in this section of the city. Jude took swig after swig from his wine skin, stumbling along the path. The clanking of armor, coins, and weaponry followed a short distance behind him.

Looking over his shoulder, Jude saw several centurions, clustered together with some of the priests. A few held torches, lighting small patches of their path. Perhaps 100 meters behind him, Jude still felt the anxious weight of their eyes on his back.

"I have to do this…" Jude recited ad nauseum. "I have to do this… I have to do this…"

Coming up over a small hill, Jude's eyes caught a silhouette, praying on their knees before a fire. Jude swallowed the lump that appeared in his throat. On he stumbled toward the fire, a short distance off the beaten path. Soft sobs, broken up by frantic mumbling, broke through the sounds of the fire popping and snapping.

Jude staggered over something as he approached Jesus. Tumbling to the ground, there was grunting, a yelp, the shuffling of robes, and several feet clamoring over to Jude.

"Jude?" came Simon's voice.

Jude looked up to find Simon, Bartholomew, and Andrew standing around him. The sobs and utterances continued by the fire.

"Hey guys," Jude slurred out. He waved to them with childish gestures.

Simon gave a look of disappointment, hanging his head as he rubbed his eyes. "Help him up," Simon ordered the other two, waving his hands as he turned and walked away. Bartholomew and Andrew both grabbed an arm. Andrew, grabbing the arm Jude had his wine skin in hand with, jumped back as wine gushed from the skin onto his clothing. Jude, Bartholomew, and Simon all laughed as Andrew attempted to wipe off the red splotch on his tunic.

"I'm going to look like the lamb led to slaughter!" Andrew shot at them.

Bartholomew reached back over, grabbing both of Jude's arms, and pulling him back up to his feet. Jude snickered as he found his bearings.

"*Why do you laugh?*" came a stoic voice behind Simon.

The men turned to find Jesus staring at them through the tops of his eyes. Looking like a rat from the sewers, his hair disheveled, face puffy and moist, his clothing stained with sweat.

"Do you find humor in our circumstance?" Jesus asked.

Jude's face turned mournful, his mouth opened and closed as he struggled to articulate his thoughts.

"My brother," Jesus said. "You're hurting."

Jude's mouth trembled, and he dropped the wine skin. Placing his hand on Jude's shoulders, Jesus pulled him in and embraced him. Jude wrapped his arms around Jesus, grimacing as tears flowed freely down his face.

"It's okay," Jesus sobbed. "You shouldn't carry this weight by yourself."

Jude ground his teeth from side to side, locking his lips tight to not allow his pain out. To not put his anguish on Jesus. "I forgive you," he whispered in Jude's ear.

Jude sobbed as he placed his lips on Jesus' cheek.

"There!" came a cry from behind them. "The one whom he has embraced!"

Jude turned back toward Jesus, his mouth agape. Tears gushed down his face as he walked with caution away from Jesus. Jesus turned his nose up, standing with a firm disposition as the centurions approached.

One guard approached Jesus with an outstretched hand to grab him. Jude felt an arm slide into his tunic, retrieving his knife.

"Simon, no!" cried Jesus.

Simon lunged at the guard, swiping at the centurion's head with the blade. The centurion, catching sight of Jude mere seconds before, turned his head as Simon's downward slash caught him. With a burst of crimson, the blade connected right above the guard's left ear, dragging down and across his jawline. The blade exited his flesh, leaving a strip of tissue hanging from the corner of his jaw like uncooked bacon. His teeth and gumline exposed, it looked like those creepy pictures in the anatomy books from Jude's mother's college biology text books. Except for all the blood and mess. Simon's blade also left a gash across the officer's chest, exposing a trail of blood that seeped with unexpected speed into his clothing.

Screaming, the man struggled to place his skin back up to his face. Every touch and movement appeared to magnify the intensity of his pain. Other officers descended upon Simon, clutching him by his arms, forcing him to drop the knife.

"No!" cried Jude. "No, you promised me."

"We promised you no one would be harmed if your followers cooperated," screamed one of the Pharisees.

Simon looked over his shoulder at Jude. "This is how it happens?" he demanded.

Andrew and Bartholomew both turned to Jude, looking at him with horrified eyes.

"Wait," Jesus called to them.

Turning to Jesus, the others witnessed him approach the guard whose face had been mutilated. Kneeling before him, another Roman withdrew a sword. Jesus held up his hands to show he had no weapons. The injured guard grunted and cried as he stressed over his wounds.

"My brother," Jesus whispered to him.

The man looked up, uncertainty and disbelief in his eyes. With a gentle hand, Jesus lifted the skin flap up to the man's face. Jesus whispered something to himself, all but discernible as speech to the others. The centurion groaned and let out incensed sounds as he appeared to struggle. The red stains in his uniform disappeared, as if evaporated by the sun.

After a moment, Jesus pulled away, removing his hand from the man's face. The blood was gone, the flap of skin remained attached to his face. Several of the centurions stood and stared. Jesus stood up, glaring at Simon. "He who lives by the sword," he said, "shall die by it."

Simon wept as the soldiers held him.

"Forget the youth," one of the Pharisees shouted. "Give us who we came for!"

Dropping Simon, who collapsed into a heap, they approached Jesus. Pulling out a rope, they tied his hands behind his back, securing another rope between his feet with enough slack for him to walk at a reasonable pace. Jesus looked back at his friends and brothers with a sorrowful look. The centurions pushed him forward, jeering at him.

As the Romans and Pharisees disappeared over the hillside, the men's weeping became the only audible noise. Apart from the fire crackling, it was met with silence. Jude stumbled forward, finding a full wine skin resting on the ground. Scooping it up, Jude trekked forward, uncorking the container.

"Judas!" cried Simon from behind.

Bringing the skin to his lips, Jude looked over his shoulder. The dark silhouette of Simon ran down the hill, stumbling as he fought for stable footing. Jude smiled, swallowing the bitter sting of the wine.

Kicking rocks past Jude as he approached, Simon called again to him. "Will you stop, Judas?" he begged.

"Why?" asked Jude, wiping his mouth. "I've served my purpose."

The running had slowed to a light jog, as Jude felt a hand grasp at his shoulder. He turned, walking backward as he sipped from his wine skin.

"Where are you going?" asked Simon.

"I'm going to watch," Jude said.

"What?" gasped Simon. "Are you crazy? If they see you there, they'll kill you."

"Exactly," said Jude, turning back to face the road.

"My brother," cried Simon. "I need you now. Everyone is hiding. Mother is... I don't know where. Wherever the girls are. Thomas has disappeared. I-I need you."

"Then follow me," Jude said, reaching his hand back.

They walked a few meters further, and Jude stopped when Simon didn't take his hand. Looking back at Simon, the lights from the court-yard started to illuminate trace amounts of their features. Young Simon, so driven, so loyal. Who better to found the church?

"Simon," Jude said, attempting to lock eyes in the shadows.

Simon rubbed at his cheeks, clenching his jaw.

"Brother, do not fret," Jude reassured him, placing his hand along his lower back. "You were Jesus' rock, now I need you to be mine."

Simon's mouth formed into a stern scowl, pursing his lips.

Placing his hands on the back of Simon's neck, Jude brought their foreheads together. The tips of their noses brushed against each other. Both closed their eyes.

"Breathe," Jude said. And they both took in a large breath, exhaling through their mouths. "It is your choice what you do," He said, releasing Simon's neck. "Just know that, whatever you choose to do, you have a long and prosperous mark to still leave on our story."

Simon smiled up at him, rubbing his arm.

"And if you promise to be my rock," Jude continued, "then I'll be yours."

Simon looked at his feet, twiddling his toes and rocking on his heels.

"Okay," said Simon, his head snapping up. "I'll go."

Smiling, Jude offered his wine skin to Simon. "Here," he said, bringing the container to Simon's lips. "This helps."

Simon took the skin, swallowing more than he intended. Keeling over, Simon coughed and hacked, with a loud belch rocketing from his mouth. Jude laughed, slapping him on the back.

"Be careful," Jude chuckled at his disoriented brother. "If you can walk on water, you're not allowed to drown on wine."

20

Jude and Simon stumbled into the courtyard. To their surprise, it was alive and pulsing with human activity. There appeared to be no shops open, no money changers, no livestock.

"What's that about?" Simon asked, throwing his arm up. He pointed toward a stage where several Roman guards stood watch. Torches lit by four corners; two figures stood in the center.

"I can't see who they are," Jude said, squinting.

"That looks like another Roman," said Simon. "He's showing more skin, so he must be more important."

Simon took another mouthful of wine, passing it back to Jude. Shaking the wine skin, Jude upended it, sucking away at the final drops. With a flick of his wrist, he sent the skin hurtling like a stone, skipping across the ground. As they marched closer to the stage, Jude started to recognize some of the faces of people who shifted their gaze from the stage for a moment. Jude saw the men and women that placed palms before Jesus as he rode in on the foal. People that had protected him when he overturned the tables.

"Jude," whispered Simon. "What's happening?"

Looking back, Jude saw an arsenal of centurions, swords drawn, lining up behind them. From all sides, centurions closed around the group of onlookers. Many were in their sleeping attire. Everyone had a cautious frightened look on their face. Some held children that cried. The Romans shoved some of the stragglers, grunting commands to "hurry up!"

"Filthy vermin," they bemoaned the audience.

"Get to it!" others called.

A hard jab into his back, and Jude jumped forward as he whipped around.

"What are you going to do about it, Jew?" an enraged centurion bent forward, peering into Jude's eyes.

Jude's arms shot up in surrender, turning forward and rushing to join the rest of the crowd.

"Pilate," Simon said.

"What?" asked Jude.

"It's Pilate," Simon repeated. "On the stage."

"Who's the guy with leprosy next to him?" Jude sneered.

"Do not joke," Simon demanded. "Those people suffer like any other."

"Simon!" Jude stopped him. "Listen!"

It was faint, but they both heard a rhythmic chant. It was almost indecipherable, until they saw the guards threaten the witnesses along the outer ring. First some screams and grunts, and then it was distinct.

"*Rex Iudaeorum… Rex Iudaeorum… Rex Iudaeorum…*"

Some swords pointed over the back rows and gestured at various individuals. Like the volume knob had been cranked up, in a wave, the chant was called out by everyone before the stage.

"*Rex Iudaeorum… Rex Iudaeorum… Rex Iudaeorum…*"

"King of the Jews…" Simon whispered.

"No…" Jude muttered. "Jesus…"

Quaking as he stood beside Pilate, Jesus' flesh was blistered, torn, and bruised. The wounds fresh, Jesus' skin was stained a deep vermillion. A purple rag had been draped over his shoulders, a crown of thorns impaling his scalp. One of Jesus' eyes had been jabbed by a thorn. It was swollen over, a red dripping circle surrounding the spike still embedded in his eye. He drooled as he sobbed before the crowd.

"Here is your king," Pilate hollered, raising a hand to silence the chant. "Here is the king of the Jews."

All stood in unified panic. Like a telekinetic bond, each appeared to follow an unspoken fear of moving. The fear being they might be next. Pacing along the front of the stage, Pilate looked among the faces in the crowd. His attire demanding respect for his political authority. The haloed wings, a crown of sorts he wore as Prefect, implied a sense of divinity. His face commanded submission.

"This king," Pilate continued, "rode into your city in an act of mockery toward Roman authority. The authority that protects you from outside forces. Need I remind you of your stay in Egypt?" Turning to the other half of the group, Pilate raised his fist. "Or Babylon?" he cried.

The audience wailed in response. Some prayed; several women wept.

"You dare bite the hand that feeds you?" Pilate demanded. "You would dare serve a king that questions the good will, and generous religious freedoms, of the great Caesar?"

Several shook their heads.

"Then why do my dutiful guards report seeing so many of your faces there today?" Pilate called out. "Why did my men report seeing all of you shout things like 'all hail' to this miscreant? Laying palm branches, in a mockery of the roses we throw for our military heroes? How dare you." He shook his finger at the Jews, making a *tsk* sound as his finger bounced back and forth.

"As disappointed as I am," Pilate continued, clasping his hands behind his back. "I am willing to offer you an opportunity to redeem yourselves, and prove your loyalty to Rome."

"Please, your grace," one person shouted. A small wave of similar calls and requests echoed through the group.

"*Of course, your grace.*"

"*We are eager to prove ourselves, your grace!*"

Turning to two centurions at the rear of the stage, Pilate nodded. They approached the rear of the stage, interlocking arms with a man who had been seated during the confrontation of the crowd. Dragging him up to the front of the stage, he was in as rough a shape as Jesus was.

Both eyes were swollen shut, his jaw broken, hanging in an odd position, covered in whip marks. One of his legs looked like it was broken. He sat at the front of the stage, swaying as he fought to sit upright.

"May I present Barabbas," Pilate said, gesturing at the mess of a man seated before him. "He is a traitor to the empire, a thief, and a murderer."

The crowd gasped. Jude recognized the sound from his mother's soap operas. These assholes were faking. They were too afraid of getting caught.

"We out number them," Jude said to Simon.

"Don't be crazy," Simon said. "They have the weapons. And we don't have a great success rate for attempts to overthrow other nations."

"This is theater," Jude continued. "This has nothing to do with betraying Rome."

"This is what I offer you," Pilate announced. "I will give you a choice of who to free. The person remaining in my custody will then be sentenced to death."

The crowd shuffled in a cautious, uncomfortable manner.

"So," concluded Pilate. "Who shall it be? Jesus, the self-proclaimed 'King of the Jews?'"

One person started to applaud, and a centurion dove into the crowd. After a mild commotion, the centurion came out grabbing a young man by his hair.

"Bartholomew!" called Simon. "It's Bartholomew!"

Bartholomew struggled, pulling at the back of the guard's knees. Chuckling, the guard unsheathed his sword. And with one swift slice, he severed Bartholomew's head.

"Fuck!" cried Jude, clutching his throat.

Blood rocketed from the neck of Bartholomew's lifeless body. The head drizzled as if the Roman had just retrieved it from a bath tub.

"Once more," Pilate said. "Who wishes for the 'King of the Jews' to be released?"

Aside from crickets chirping, not a sound was made. No one appeared to even breathe as they stood in anxious wait. Nodding, Pilate approached the haggard mess of a man at the front of the stage.

"Now who wishes for Barabbas' freedom?" Pilate called.

The Jews cried out, waving their arms in the air.

"*Free Barabbas!*"

"*Not the blasphemer!*"

"*Barabbas!*"

Pilate smirked as he approached Barabbas from behind.

"As you wish," he called. And with a forceful thrust, Pilate raised his foot and shoved Barabbas over the edge of the stage. Landing with a loud crack, the shattered man shrieked as he lay on the ground. "Now," cried Pilate. "What shall we do with our almighty king?"

Murmurs weaved in and out of the crowds, people having philosophical discussions about the meaning of life in compact narratives. Which punishment would they choose?

"*Crucify him!*" called a gruff voice from the outside of the group.

"*Yes,*" called another sandpaper voice from the other end of the group.

"*Crucify him!*" others began to chant.

Eyes within the group darted around. People cried. Jude overheard a woman pleading to God for forgiveness.

"They know not what they do…" she prayed into her hands. "They know not what they do."

"*Crucify him!*" the chant unified among the voices. It swelled in volume.

"*Crucify him!*"

The plosive consonant of the chant sounded like a fearful outburst from the crowd. A therapist Jude had seen once as a child told him that fear and anger were both secondary emotions. Maybe that's why it was so easy to mask one as the other. Raising his hands in the air to silence them, Pilate waited with an appearance of reverence and respect. Once the crowd had grown silent, Pilate lowered his hands and cleared his throat.

"As you wish," Pilate announced, a smug smirk oozing across his face.

The Jews erupted in cheers

"They're rewarding the crowd," Simon said, looking around them with panic-stricken eyes. "We need to move."

Jude moved with reluctance at Simon's behest. Looking back at the stage, he wept as he watched several centurions approach Jesus, slugging him in the stomach.

"What have I done?" Jude cried.

"*Hey you*," a woman called.

Simon and Jude both turned to see a woman glaring at them. Her hand waving in their faces.

"See," she called behind her. "I told you. It's them!"

"What?" asked Simon.

A man leaned over the woman, squinting at the men. "Yes," he hissed. "You were with him, the king there."

"No we weren't," Simon snapped.

"I'm sure you were," the woman said. "I know I saw you two around the foal."

"That wasn't us," said Simon. "We don't know him."

"Aren't you his brothers?" asked the man. "The sons of that nutty mason in Nazareth?"

"Nothing good comes from Nazareth," Simon shouted. "We do *not* know him!"

In the distance, a cock crowed. Looking over the walls of the courtyard, a pinkish-orange sunrise peeked over the edges.

"God, no," Simon cried, turning to Jude.

"You were right," Simon sobbed. "Please, brother, forgive me."

"Not now," Jude shoved him. "We need to leave."

"*Hey drunkard!*" came a deep voice at the edge of the crowd.

Jude looked up to see a centurion holding out a wine skin.

"Here's your payment," he called, tossing the skin.

Jude clasped it in his arms, holding it like an infant. Simon shook his head as he watched Jude uncork the container and guzzle the contents.

"Our brother's blood for a taste of wine," Simon wept.

21

As the wine skin emptied, Jude's memories of the time after became intermittent. Like mental time travel, his first recollection was running alongside Simon through the streets of Jerusalem. His chest heavy, part of him felt alive for once. He found himself acting out the dreams he'd had as a child, living out a wild adventure. This was history. This was a moment in time that historians would scale over for centuries. People would wonder what was going through his mind, what he felt, his mental state. All he could think was, *At last I'm free*...

Jude's next memory was of him and Simon, going door to door in search of their family. Passing the wine skin as they crisscrossed through dirt roads with Jewish housing. They giggled with each slammed door or holler from a freshly woken mother with children asleep. It felt like the school boy mischief he never had a chance to live out. Thanks to the Christian kids in the community. Thanks to looking like a stereotypical Jew. Simon understood him. Simon loved him. Simon mourned with him.

Another memory came to Jude. This time he was pleading with a man to release Simon. He remembered saying, "*Please don't choke him. We're just lost. We're looking for our family.*"

"*Please sir,*" Jude had begged before slugging the man in the face. "*I beg you.*"

The man had stopped moving, his face a bruised and bloody pulp. Simon had dropped a long, wooden staff. Blood splattered on the ground as he ran.

Did Simon do something to him? Jude wondered. *Or did I?*

Jude's memory blurred, finding himself in a stranger's kitchen, Simon seated beside him. They had glasses with an odd tasting wine. The home owner, an old shriveled looking man with jaundiced eyes, burned an odd incense in the middle of the table. Waving the fumes into his face, the old man smiled in gratitude. He slurred his speech, not that the language he spoke was one that they understood.

Jude felt remarkable; he was so complete and at ease, such a change from how he felt every day. Even with the wine. He felt as if in a dream.

"Let's go Jude," Simon shoved him.

"But why?" asked Jude. "I'm just starting to get comfortable."

"I heard Judith," Simon said.

Jude perked up. "Okay," he said. "Let's go find her."

Jude's memory became almost non-existent. Merely snapshots of moments, flooded with intense emotions. Using someone's home to support himself, a light and loud voice came through the window as he hollered Judith's name. Simon was shoving Jude down the road, his heart racing. Heavy footsteps approached behind them.

Hearing Judith's voice. So soft, so concerned. The way she called "My Jude!" to him, it all made his heart swell. He belonged. Someone felt he was "theirs." He was wanted, needed. But then, he ruined it. The hurt and despair as he went in for a kiss, laying on the floor next to Judith.

She pulled away.

"Please," he begged her.

At first, her look was sadness. The same look she gave him when he acted like a child: scared, hurt, and wanting to make it better. Yet she realized she could do little to stop the hurt.

"Just let me show you how much I love you," Jude pleaded

"No," she said. "Not tonight, not now…"

The rage that enveloped his perspective, the sheer horror of the one who loves him most. How could she deny him in his moment of need? Did she not know what he was going through?

"Why won't you let me love you?" Jude said, perching himself over her. His hands holding her wrists.

"Please let go," she grunted, trying to move her wrists.

"Just give me a chance," he begged, tears streaming down his face.

"You're hurting me!" her voice raised.

"Stop shouting!" Jude grunted through clenched teeth.

"Jude!" she cried.

He leaned over and kissed her, attempting to silence her shouts. Her muffled yells were countered with him twisting her arms. Judith clamped down on Jude's lower lip with her teeth.

"Aah!" hollered Jude. Gibberish poured from his mouth, unable to articulate.

The muscles around Judith's jaw tensed, and blood oozed out from between her teeth. Jude's shriek swiped through the soundscape like an arrow through the ether. His hands came up and clutched Judith around the neck. Before he could tense his hands, Jude found himself on his back. Simon stood over him, swinging away at his face.

"Piece of shit!" he hollered. "You bastard!"

It didn't hurt, he remembered later. But it was disorienting, and he knew he needed to leave. Shoving Simon aside, Jude jumped up and scrambled to find the exit. As he looked around for a way out, he found himself face to face with Judith. She spat something in his face. Catching it in his hand, he gazed down to find a blood streaked lip. His lip. With the windup of a baseball pitcher, Judith swung her arm in a tight arch, connecting with Jude's jaw.

Next, Jude was on the ground, staring up at Simon. He was on the street outside of the apartment they rented. "...and if I ever see you come near our family again," Simon shouted, "I'll fucking kill you."

Looking up the roadway, numerous people peered out their windows and doors. Everyone liked gossip, and now he would be the figure catching everyone's interest the following day.

They don't know, Jude thought. *They haven't experienced what I have.*

A wineskin and a tunic were tossed out the door, landing beside him. Several onlookers "oooh'd" and made cynical comments.

Jude wept.

And then nothing.

22

The screams were the worst part.

Jude looked down the valley toward Golgotha. Three new crosses had been erected that morning, and one was, without question, Jesus. He stood atop a metal bin, abandoned by the former shepherd that once raised livestock here. The tunic Simon had thrown at him was knotted around his neck and the branch of the tree he stood beneath.

Blood streaked down Jude's jaw and throat, now covered by the tunic. Bruises littered his face, dirt crusted over old wounds with dried blood. His heart raced, but his face was stern. He sipped at his wine skin, looking out over the valley where corpses were displayed for all to see. Swallowing the remaining drops of his wine, Jude tossed the skin off to the side of the tree. Looking at the landscape around him, he smiled. The rocks below, the terrain, seemed to form in a special pattern. A message just for him. With the hill down from the tree, they appeared to rise up to meet him.

"*Soon you will rejoin us,*" he felt he heard them say. "*Return to the Earth.*"

Looking up at the sky, Jude closed his eyes and breathed through his nose. "It is over," he whispered. And with the sound of the shrieks from Golgotha punctuating the air, Jude rocked the tin back and forth. His natural biological reaction was to find balance, planting the bucket back down on its lip. With a hearty thrust, the bucket rolled out from underneath him. Awaiting the slack from the tunic, Jude was startled to find himself instead collapsing onto the ground.

Jumping up, heaving, Jude grasped at his neck. The tunic was gone. So were the screams, the hill he had been on, the bucket. Instead, he was in the front yard of his childhood home.

"What…?" Jude gasped.

"*You remember?*" came a voice behind him.

Creeping up beside Jude, the man who had claimed to be his father slid his arm over his shoulder.

"I figured you would," the man continued. "How old are you now? 33? 34?"

"I…" Jude shook his head, staring at the house. "I don't know."

"So I bet you're wondering what happened after you disappeared," the man said. "Instead of adding to their stress, your disappearance helped them collaborate and work together."

The sound of children's laughter squeaked out of the house, somewhere. Jude's head flipped as his eyes bulged in hope.

"They paid more attention to your sister, realizing how precious the time was," the man continued. "How easily it can be taken away."

The sound of laughter, heavy footprints, and a familiar, masculine voice.

"*Grampa's gonna get you!*"

Squeals and small footsteps racing somewhere in the house followed.

"They had another child a few years after your disappearance," he said. "They named him Jude."

"I was replaced," he whispered.

"It's not really their fault," the man said, turning to Jude. "They had found a body that resembled you in some way. The clothing matched what they remember you wearing, despite finding the clothes in your drawers that were found on the body as they finally cleaned out your shrine of a room. Your mother couldn't sleep for weeks after. She never brought it up because, how silly! There was a man who readily admitted to the crime. He confessed to doing unspeakable things to you, and you specifically. Why would an innocent man make those things up?"

174

Jude sat, mesmerized by the sounds coming from the house.

"She questioned whether you were actually dead," the man went on. "No one else did. She was sure that something wasn't right, but she knew, rightly so, that others would call her crazy.

"Your sister and brother became scholars in their fields, excelling in string theory and quantum computing, respectively. Your siblings both recognized your parents trying to have you reenter the picture through your brother, but they inevitably gave up when they realized it was re-traumatizing your sister. Your brother also endured some undue stress. Learning from their past mistakes, they allowed both of your siblings to explore what was important to them."

"I got in the way," Jude muttered.

"I don't know that I'd go that far," said the man. "But it was because of your disappearance that your family became so strong."

The front door opened, both men looking up with wide eyes.

"*Grampa, look!*" came a small voice from the door way.

A boy, no older than four or five, looked at Jude and the man. His short, crew cut style, blond hair, red shorts, and crocs. Jude recognized the Flash superhero insignia on the tank top the boy wore.

Walking out through the doorway, Jude recognized his father almost at once. His hair now white, sporting a long, wizard-like beard, everything else about him was the same. The inquisitive, one-eyebrow look when he was suspicious or knew he was lying. A Boston Bruins hoodie with blue jeans and loafers on. Jude sniffed, trying to hold back his tears.

"Hey," called his father. "Buddy you look hurt. Do you need me to call the hospital?"

Jude glanced back and forth between the man and his father. Swallowing the lump in his throat, Jude shook his head.

"Hey Dad," came a woman's voice. "What's going on?"

Coming out behind his father, Jude looked upon a full-grown Sarah. Wearing librarian glasses, a tank top, and leggings, she gave a curious look to the men on her father's front lawn.

175

"Who are these guys?" she asked.

"I don't know," said their father, shrugging his shoulders.

"Do you need help?" she called to them.

"Sarah," cried Jude, slapping his hands over his mouth. The grime on his face made him feel sick. How could this be the way he's reunited with his family?

"Mommy, who is that?" asked the small boy. "Why does he know your name?"

"*Everything alright?*" came a man's voice.

Jude froze.

Out walked a cleaner, well-groomed, younger version of himself. The likeness was almost uncanny. Sarah looked back and forth between her younger and older brother.

"Yeah," she said with hesitation, pulling the child closer to her.

"Who are you sir?" Jude's father called to him.

All eyes were on Jude. The people he loved, that he had never met before, yet he felt such a desperate yearning to embrace them. That was not what this was about, Jude realized. Looking up at his family, his brother, father, sister, and nephew, Jude had not been brought back here to reunite with them. This was a means to an end.

"They were better off without me," Jude whispered.

The man grunted in agreement, nodding his head.

"Who *are* you, mister?" called the little boy.

His mother tried to silence him, placing her hand over his mouth.

Jude smiled as he made eye contact with the young boy. Shaking his head, Jude finally spoke. "No one special," he said. "Just a random bad guy."

As if the floor had ripped out from underneath himself, Jude's heart jumped as he tumbled in a free fall toward the Earth. With wind whipping through his clothes, pulling his hair back, Jude struggled to find his bearings. He had just enough time to look down and see himself fall from the tree, and disappear in a flash, before meeting the rocks below.

About the Author

Matthew O'Neil is an activist, theologian, and teacher. He has an MA in theology from Saint Michael's College, and he is a certified Humanist chaplain and celebrant. He is the author of *You Say That I Am, What the Bible Really Does (and Doesn't) Say About Sex, After Life,* and *Attrition.* He lives in Charlotte, North Carolina.